About the Author

A. V. Hagelund is a young author who always loved romance and storytelling. She was often thought of as the gifted child, with talents for literature and creative thinking, and was always recognized as the best writer in her class. Throughout her school years, she found herself immersing into the comfort of reading and decided that she herself wanted to go down the route of writing. From there on out, she started on her first ever book, and worked on it every chance she got. It was tedious and hard, and she had to start over multiple times, but finally in 2023 she reached a satisfying result.

A Flower in Chains

A. V. Hagelund

A Flower in Chains

Olympia Publishers
London

www.olympiapublishers.com
OLYMPIA PAPERBACK EDITION

Copyright © A. V. Hagelund 2024

The right of A. V. Hagelund to be identified as author of
this work has been asserted in accordance with sections 77 and 78 of
the Copyright, Designs and Patents Act 1988.

All Rights Reserved

No reproduction, copy or transmission of this publication
may be made without written permission.
No paragraph of this publication may be reproduced,
copied or transmitted save with the written permission of the publisher,
or in accordance with the provisions
of the Copyright Act 1956 (as amended).

Any person who commits any unauthorized act in relation to
this publication may be liable to criminal
prosecution and civil claims for damage.

A CIP catalogue record for this title is
available from the British Library.

ISBN: 978-1-80439-751-0

This is a work of fiction.
Names, characters, places and incidents originate from the writer's
imagination. Any resemblance to actual persons, living or dead, is
purely coincidental.

First Published in 2024

Olympia Publishers
Tallis House
2 Tallis Street
London
EC4Y 0AB

Printed in Great Britain

Dedication

I dedicate this book to my beloved grandmother, Karen Hagelund, who lent me the money to fulfill my dreams of publishing this book.

Acknowledgments

Thank you to my biggest supporters during this process and some of my closest friends, who helped shape the story into what it is today. Linda Hui Mortensen, Ethan Magleby, Søren Haandbæk, Benjamin Astro Hviid, Chance Strange Storm, my mother and father, and other family members believing in my passion and storytelling.

Chapter 1

An Unwanted Invitation

The lime green leaves hang down around her. Birds were humming their last song in the background, signaling the day's end, and the sun was slowly disappearing behind the horizon.

These moments were some of her favorites. No servants swarming around her, no noble women whispering behind her back, and no expectations or pressure on her shoulders.

This was the best part of her chaotic life. Just sitting down on the well-maintained bench, by the pond, listening to all the things around her.

Today in particular had been rough. Her sister Elniba and some of her friends had been following her around all day and had, as always, been mocking her about her appearance.

Especially her dress.

It was a dark, maroon purple, matching her hair. Very simply styled with a slim upper half and a skirt, lazily falling down to the ground.

Elniba had said, it made her look like those old ladies, you would see out on the street, trying to imitate the nobles. She knew it wasn't anything to take seriously, but she couldn't shake it. For a long time now, her older sister had been talking down to her. Blaming things on her, being mean and just taking every opportunity to damage her already nonexistent confidence.

At least, she could be at peace here.

She stumbled upon the pond when she was around eleven. She had never been in that part of the garden before, and it had looked completely abandoned. Only a few pieces of porcelain scattered around on the ground and a mossy bench had been the only evidence of previous usage. She later asked the gardeners if they could do anything to save the spot, and the very next week, it looked wonderful. The dying flowers looked lavish, and the pond had been cleaned from algae. The gardeners had put up small oil lanterns, in the tree-branches and the bench had been cleared for all moss.

The best part though, was that only she and the gardeners knew about it. And of course, Lilly, her maid.

It was a safe space for her where no one would find her, nor bother her. A personal paradise.

She opened her eyes slowly and looked out over the water. The duck and her ducklings were swimming around as always and she noticed how big they had gotten. Soon they would leave their mother, to live a life of freedom in another pond somewhere out in the world. She envied them.

Freedom was the only thing she would never have. Money and privilege, sure, but never the power to decide when, where or how she would live.

All her life had been focused on etiquette and the court, being held in one place by her father, and not even able to choose her own dinner. The future didn't look any brighter. Soon her father would find her a suitable husband for his own political gain, and she would be stuck yet again, only with a change of scenery.

It was hell in her eyes. So, for now she would continue to sneak down to the pond, as long as it was possible.

"Lady Aimee!" someone called from across the field. She

turned around in surprise to see Lilly, running down from the main path. She was carrying what looked to be a small piece of paper in her right hand.

Lilly had been her personal maid for a year now. She had been assigned to her after Aimee had outgrown her nanny and instead received a personal servant.

She was a small, compact girl with light brown hair and beautiful blue eyes. She was normally quite beautiful, although in that moment, she looked more like an exhausted aunt than a young maid. It was only natural after having run the big distance from the mansion.

"What's wrong?" Aimee asked worriedly and stood up to greet the maid.

She finally slowed down, curtsied quickly, and handed her the peace of paper. "From the Duke," she blurted out. Lilly handed her the small piece of paper and went to the bench to sit down for a moment. Normally, it was impolite for a servant to sit without permission, but Aimee didn't like the formality, so she had told Lilly to do as she pleased, when no one else was around.

She looked down on the paper.

Aimee.
See me in my office, soon as possible.
– Sir Erlan.

Short and direct. As one could expect.

She looked down at Lilly who had somewhat recovered from her long run. Aimee hadn't been summoned by her father in weeks. This must've been of importance. She rushed from her hideout, leaving Lilly behind on the bench, moving up the steep hill and through the small forest until she reached the main flower gardens.

Once there and in view of all the guards and servants she slowed down and moved with the grace and elegance expected of the Archduke's daughter.

She went through the big glass doors leading to the main hall of the mansion, and steadily made her way through the long and beautiful corridors, decorated with warm colors and the most luxurious pieces of art. Her father had a keen eye for appearance so nothing less could be expected.

Finally, she made it to her father's chambers, where she showed the piece of paper to the guard. The Archduke had made it a principle that you could only enter if you had been summoned with a personal invite from him. To prevent unnecessary distractions probably.

The guard approved of the paper and opened the dark oak door for her. Inside were bookshelves covering all of the walls. Two couches and a table were placed in the middle of the room, making a small area for relaxing and casual conversation. All around the floor were books stacked in tall piles about warfare, politics, and taxes. The entire room was messy, because her father had banned maids from entering and cleaning without permission.

In the other end of the room, in front of a giant window looking out over the garden, was her father, sitting at his desk with papers scattered all over it.

He looked good for his age. Tall and with nicely combed-back hair, that was the same color as her sisters. A sandy blond with few white strips that shined in the sun's last light behind him.

His light-green, cold, and stone hard eyes were in contrast to hers which were a lime almost turquoise color. She had inherited her eyes from her mother. That and her hair was the only thing she had left her with, before she passed away in childbirth. Her birth.

Her father despised her for it.

Before moving further into the room, she bowed gracefully as she had done thousands of times.

"You called me, Father?" she asked, waiting for him to call her over.

He made a small hand movement without looking up from the papers on his desk. She silently moved through the mess without anything falling over.

She stood in front of the desk and once again waited for her father to speak.

"We have been invited to a party at the royal palace, in Tessas," he said in a monotone voice. He handed Aimee the paper in his hand and true enough, it was a letter with the royal symbol.

To the Archduke of Edenran, Sir Erlan Achillea, in Leirath.

You and your two lovely daughters have been invited to the Crown Prince Maxim Istatis' masquerade ball, at the royal Withall Keep Palace on the 19th-22nd June.

You will arrive at the palace on the 19th and be given your own private quarters. The next day on the 20th the party will be held in the ballroom on the first floor. All are required to wear masks covering at least their eyes and nose.

The 21st will be a relaxing day to enjoy the palace grounds and in the afternoon of the 22nd you will return home.

It would be a pleasure having the family Achillea represented at the ball.

From his highness crown prince Maxim Istatis.

That was in two days.

Aimee looked to her father in confusion.

He took a long, deep breath before he spoke. "I have important business in the south at the time of the party," he said, irritated. "And your sister will also be away, meeting her future husband Archduke Maulus Aquil in the Oldea. And that leaves you." He finally looked up from the papers. Still the same hard and cold eyes.

"I'm not quite sure I follow…?" she said carefully.

"As the only available member of our family, you will attend the party, representing all of the Edenran Duchy," he said quietly.

Her eyes went big. Never had he entrusted her with such a task. To represent a noble family was a big honor. And the thought of him finally acknowledging the fact that she could manage such affairs was the biggest recognition she had ever received from him.

She nodded in silence, still with surprise and happiness sprinkled all over her face. But it quickly fainted when she saw the small hint of disgust in the duke's eyes. Just as suddenly as she had gone flying, she was sent crashing down to earth again. His feelings towards her definitely hadn't changed. He still despised her…

She bowed politely and kept her eyes on the floor.

"It would be an honor," she said quietly. His expression hardened.

"I expect this to go perfectly," he said harshly. "If you mess up the event, you will cast shame on our good name, and I will not stand for that kind of embarrassment, you hear me, girl?" He was clearly angry now. Simply the thought of her attending this event, sent him spiraling.

"Of course, Father…" she said.

He took another deep breath through. "Who knows? Maybe you'll finally find a soothing husband and be useful to me…"

No comments.

"Was that all?" she asked, without a hint of sorrow in her voice.

"No. I've prepared a dress and a mask for you, for the masquerade. You will take off for the palace tomorrow evening and arrive in the afternoon on the nineteenth," he said it quick and sharply to make sure everything was clear to her. "This will be your official introduction into high society, so I advise you to keep a low profile. You are dismissed."

She bowed, "Thank you, Father."

She started heading towards the door, but as she reached for the handle her father spoke again.

"Aimee." She turned around and faced him. "Do not make a fool of me…" he warned.

She bowed her head slightly.

"Of course not, Father."

And as she walked out of the door she didn't bother to say goodbye.

Aimee woke up the next morning with a headache.

That boy had appeared in her dreams again. The one with the sparkling blue eyes, staring down on her from the side of her bed. His presence would usually calm her down, but yesterday's chaos with packing, planning, getting the carriages and horses ready, and all the other stuff she had to think about, had left her completely beaten down.

Today's schedule wasn't any better. First there was breakfast in her room, followed by dress fitting, inspections of the carriages and finally having to actually depart for the palace. The journey would take one and a half days and she knew it would be bumpy.

The roads around the Edenran Duchy needed repairs badly, so it would be a very uncomfortable ride.

Lilly hadn't woken her up yet, so she decided to stay in bed and enjoy the quiet for a little longer.

But alas, she didn't get much peace, before she heard a knock on the door. "Lady Aimee, it's Lilly." She heard the maid say. More than anything Aimee wanted to yell at her to go away, but she decided with herself that it wasn't very lady-like.

Instead, she made a weird grunting noise that invited the girl in.

Lilly opened the door and the light from the hall burned her eyes. She turned around in the bed but couldn't escape the sun when Lilly pulled the giant curtains to the side.

In a desperate attempt to escape it all she hid under the soft polyester covers of her bed.

"Now, my Lady, there's no time to snooze, you have a long day ahead of you. The chef prepared your breakfast, with boiled eggs and that special porridge you like. With honey, of course. I'll place it at the table for you." She went back into the hallway and pulled in her special cart, which was packed with three dishes of delicious-smelling food. She placed it on the beautifully carved table and that alone was enough to get Aimee out of her soft and warm covers.

"I'll be back in thirty minutes to help you get dressed, okay?" she asked in a calm demeanor.

"Uhm, Lilly?"

"Yes, my Lady?" she asked.

"Could you bring up something for headaches, like tea or medicine?" Aimee asked her, still half asleep.

"Of course, my Lady." Lilly quickly disappeared out into the hallway, not even making a sound as she took the cart with her.

Aimee looked around in her room.

Everything was now nicely lit and bright. She still had trouble adjusting her eyes to the light filling the clean white room, after having spent so many years in the small child's room she moved out of last year. The brown furniture and dusty corners had been replaced with a room almost fit for a Duchess.

Her new room had both office space, a proper marble fireplace and several small nooks where she could sit and enjoy her books.

The walls were covered in bookshelves just like her father's office, except the books here were about fantasy, adventure, and romance. There was also a single shelf with politics, but that kind of reading didn't interest her. The floor beneath her bed and the couches was covered by a royal blue carpet that matched the curtains. On the right side of the walls were giant windows looking out into the forest of the north, and a balcony was placed right in the middle.

Her sizable bed was comfortable and did its job well, and also fit the overall decorations.

Purple flowers were placed in white vases around the room creating a nice contrast to the blue. It was a room worthy of a princess, and yet it was just for Aimee.

She also had a bathroom in the far end of the room and of course a walk-in closet for her day-to-day attire.

It had been a big step up from her old childhood bedroom, but her father probably only moved her, after an acquaintance of his had complained about the size of the old room on her behalf.

She stepped out of the bed and slipped on her morning attire, which was a white rope with small, embroidered flowers around the edges.

She sat down, and as the smell had suggested, the food looked absolutely delicious. She wasted no time digging in, but still tried to look elegant, as she had been taught her entire life.

Just as she was done eating, Lilly knocked on the door and came in with a beautiful white dress.

Lilly helped getting her into the slim fitting bodice and it took a while for her to button up the back. But the end result was worthy of a royal title. A white gown with a thin skirt made it look weightless on her.

The sleeves were light and fell in pretty curves around her arms. Around the neckline and down the skirt were embroidered golden leaves ending in a golden hem around the bottom.

After she had squeezed down into the small thing, Lilly sat her down in front of a small make-up table inside the walk-in closet and started putting Aimee's hair up in a fairy-like ponytail with hair hanging down beneath it.

For her make-up it was a simple concoction of a red lipstick and a bit of blush on the cheeks.

Finally, she was done.

The rest of the morning went quicker than expected. She was standing outside of the carriage and was about to get in when a small trumpet salute started playing.

She turned around and shockingly saw her father walking down the stairs of the front door.

She had always thought it was stupid, how he insisted on such a salute, everywhere he went. It was probably just to make him feel like a royal.

He walked up to her, wearing a dusty-blue cape, contrasting his green eyes, and with two servants following behind him. He stopped only a foot's length before her, and his posture was menacing.

"Father, to what do I owe the honor?" she asked in an almost trembling voice. She hated that she showed that kind of fear toward him.

The Archduke of Edenran said nothing for the longest time. But suddenly he leaned in, far beyond a distance they had ever had before, and whispered in her ear: "*Do not make a fool of me.*"

Harsh and cold.

She sighed while awkwardly fiddling with her hands.

"As I said Father, of course not."

He leaned back again, still standing right in front of her, like a wall.

"Good."

He turned around and started walking back. Not even a farewell. She saw him disappearing back into the giant mansion.

She would not disappoint. She swore on her mother's grave that she would make him proud.

And then she was off, for the Withall Keep Palace.

Chapter 2

White Walls and Blue Eyes

Aimee's back was sore. It had been such a long time since she had traveled anywhere, and she could clearly feel that the roads were even more unforgiving than she had remembered.

But at last, they had arrived, and she hadn't needed to change to horseback, through the forests, canyons and other treacherous terrain.

She had been able to see Withall Keep's shining towers from miles away, but now that they had left the forest and was on their way through the gates, she could clearly see why this was called The Palace of Dreams.

It reached far into the sky with walls as white as the new fallen snow in December. The roof was made out of what looked to be pure gold, and the four main towers stretched so high up into the sky it made them look like stars from afar.

Giant windows covered much of the walls letting in the outside light, and the sight was almost blinding in the afternoon sun.

The gardens surrounding the palace were perfectly maintained with all kinds of flowers and trees creating intricate patterns on the ground. There were five impressive fountains sprinkled around the corners of the garden, with one in the center of the main courtyard.

She had heard many stories of the breathtaking palace, and

it turned out to be even grander than she had expected it to. The carriage finally stopped outside of the main doors and Lilly rushed out to prepare a small step for Aimee to step on in the high heels. It took all of her willpower and self-control not to stretch her sore limbs, when both her feet sat sturdy on the ground. It wasn't very lady-like cracking your bones in public, for some stupid reason.

In front of the giant wooden doors stood a small lineup of what looked like an old lady in a maid uniform, two actual maids, a butler, and another man, who probably had the unfortunate job of having to carry all her bags to her chambers.

The lady stepped forward and formally introduced herself.

"Welcome, Lady Aimee Achillea. It is an honor having you here with us. I promise that we will take exceptional good care of you," she said, "my name is Renda, and I am the head maid here at the estate. These," she pointed to the two maids, "will be your personal servants for your entire stay. If you find them unqualified we will immediately find you someone else. They will take care of your daily attire, schedule, and the cleaning of your chambers of course. This is Sheldy, your lead maid. Renda said and pointed to one of the women. She looked middle aged and experienced, so Aimee knew she was in good hands. "Sheldy will make sure everything is managed with utmost care and precision. We hope to make your stay at the Withall Keeps Palace as comfortable as possible."

Aimee was impressed with the warmth and hospitality in her voice, something she wasn't used to back home. It was clear to her that Renda must have been very passionate about her status and power in the palace household.

"Thank you for the wonderful welcome," Aimee said. "If it isn't too much of a hassle I would like to retire to my chambers immediately and have a tour of the palace later if there isn't anything planned already." Renda nodded, approving of her plan. "I would also like my maid Lilly to lead the two others as she knows me and my needs more than anyone."

"Well of course, my Lady. It is only natural for someone to trust their own companion more, than two completely new faces. Please, follow me to your chambers." She bowed and proceeded to lead the way up the stairs and through the massive doors.

She took a deep breath. This was her first time entering the doors of the palace alone. Once she stepped through them, she was completely alone. Unknown ground.

She sighed and started moving her legs, one at a time, up the beautiful stairs.

The giant main hall looked like something from an actual dream. The giant marble stones used in everything from walls, to roof, to the floors. Massive granite pillars lined the seemingly endless corridor, and along the floor laid a blood red rug with patterns of gold.

Noble ladies and gentlemen walked through the halls in expensive clothes and with extraordinary hair and jewels. They didn't bother to admire any of the beautiful decor, which had probably cost more than a fortune. They were like art pieces all on their own, helping the palace come to life.

The walls were covered in portraits of previous regents and battles, from long before her time. She recognized some faces, like Princess Sofeel and King Aldrick, but most of them were foreign to her.

A portrait of a young boy caught her eyes, as she followed Renda through the entrance hall.

He had blonde, almost white hair and menacing dark blue eyes. A lazy smile rested on his thin face and gave him an unnerving appearance. His attire was of the royal families' colors, blue, gold, and white and he was sitting laid back on a chair way too big for his size.

And it was dark. Not the hall it was placed in, the painting. Like the artist had put a thin layer of black paint over it and left the background to be nothing but void.

Eerie, she thought to herself.

She looked at the nametag describing the image's content.

Crown Prince Maxim Istatis II, future king of Oplia and Archduke of Slemith, eight years old.

So this was the famous Prince Maxim. He was known along the lands for his extensive spending of money, parties, and unpopularity amongst the nobles and the people. Was he to be their future king?

He was nothing but a spoiled brat, she bet.

A sour taste spread throughout her mouth, like poison.

"My Lady? Is everything all right?" The head maid asked, from a bit further down the hall.

"Ah yes—" she stuttered. "Of course. Sorry, I must be more tired than I thought," Aimee answered and put a hand to her head. The headache had only gotten worse over the bumping ride there.

"Yes, of course. Please follow me to your room. Quickly my Lady," Renda said.

She led Aimee up the main stairs to the second floor. There they walked down a long corridor of rooms and noble apartments, until they reached her own chambers for the time being. Her family's official colors, dark and light pink, were prominently painted on top of the door. Their signifying crest, a sword crossing a pickaxe, representing the overseeing of the export of crystals and minerals, from the mountains in Edenran, was carved into the wood of the wooden door.

Renda opened it up revealing a beautiful entrance hall with a grant table standing in the middle. On it was a pretty vase with the signifying achillea flowers showcased in a beautiful bouquet. Giant windows leading out to the balcony on the other side let the now setting sun in, light up the entire place in a deep orange color. The floor was made of some of the finest stones she had ever seen, with an array of white and black forming intricate patterns. She didn't know any of their names, but she was amazed by them either way.

There were two doors on either side of the room. She walked to the right one and opened it up to a giant study with bookshelves, an elegant office desk, a dining table, and a couch area before a magnificent fireplace, surprisingly made of what looked like polished wood.

The entire left wall was made of glass looking out over the palace gardens and on the right side were what looked to be a door to a bathroom.

She walked out of the room, not feeling the need to investigate it further at that moment. She made her way to the other side of the hall, to the left door and found herself standing in a grant bedroom.

The floor was made out of a beautiful kind of oak, and the ceiling looked to be made of white limestone. The king-sized bed covers, and the carpets covering the floor was a dark pink color like her hair, and yet again were bookshelves a big part of the decorations. This time the right wall was all glass, and in one of the corners was a cute little chair and a table, probably for relaxing and to enjoy the view of the gardens.

To the left were four additional doors. Two of them leading

to spacious rooms, with the same kinds of scaled down furniture. Probably for children or other guests. The third room was an empty walk-in closet, soon to be filled with what little clothes she had brought. And the fourth door was an appropriate bathroom with yet again, grand features, such as a porcelain bathtub with golden lion's feet. Tiles, colored in a pretty light blue, were covering the walls and purple achilleas in a vase on top of a counter pulled it all together. A toilet, and a sink was also there, and it was, of course, up to the expected standard of the royal palace.

"Is everything to your liking, my Lady?" Renda asked from the door.

"Ah yes. Everything is exceptional. Thank you," she answered.

"Would you like to hear the rest of today's schedule?" she asked in a nice warm tone.

Aimee gave a slight nod and started walking around the bedroom taking in every single precious detail.

"Well, right now and for the next two hours you are allowed to do as you please. At seven-thirty dinner will be served, either in the great dining hall, or you can choose to have it sent up here for a private dinner. The royal family will not be attending the meal in the great hall. Afterwards there will once again be time for free roaming of the palace. Do note though, that the third floor is off limits as it is the royal family's private floor. Also, all doors with iron handles are not allowed to guests. Those are only for servants or officers to use. There will be an entertaining play performed at the outside amphitheater to the north wall. It starts at nine."

"Thank you," Aimee said calmly. "That will be all for now. I would like all of my luggage in the front hall where the maids can unpack for me. You are free to go," she continued in a calming voice. She wanted to show as much gratitude for the head maid as possible, even though it wasn't common practice to thank a mere servant.

"And the tour?" Renda asked. "Shall I arrange for someone to show you around when you are done with your rest, my Lady?"

Aimee thought about it for a time. "No, that won't be necessary. I think I would like to explore this incredible place on my own," she explained and smiled to the old lady.

"Well, of course. I will leave you to it then." Renda bowed deeply and rushed out of the room again.

Aimee took a deep breath. She did it. She had traveled all alone from her home in Edenran as the sole representative of her small family. This was her chance to show how useful she could be. Her fists clenched by the thought of a recognition she had never received before, but only read about in her many books.

Lilly and the two other girls were out in the hall, already unpacking all of her clothes and other belongings. They were very efficient, having already finished two of her suitcases.

"Girls," she called out loud. The three, almost like dogs, dropped everything and lined up in front of her with incredible speed. Even Lilly who was usually nonchalant, seemed to be on her best game, almost as to prove her worth to the other two. "Good. Now what are your names again? I want to be on the best term with all of you," she said, while nodding to the two new faces. They looked a bit unsure at each other.

"My name is Sheldy," the oldest looking one said, "and this is Linari. We've been working together for two years by now."

"Excellent. And this is of course, Lilly. You've already met so I suppose you have nothing much to discuss." Aimee pointed to the girl and the three exchanged smiles. "For your first task, could you please loosen up my corset? I plan on resting for a bit, and that is utterly impossible with this thing." She laughed and immediately they were all over her like vultures, taking off her outer layers, and loosening up the strings on her back. It was truly the greatest feeling she knew. Taking off the tight thing and letting everything loose. She could finally breathe again.

"Thank you. Now please leave me for a while, so I can take a nap. Wake me up in half an hour."

"Of course, my Lady," Lilly said, and just as fast as they all arrived they were gone again.

Another deep breath. She was here now. At the royal palace, all alone. A kind of peace fell over her. She never actually thought she would get so far. Aimee had always thought that the day she arrived here was the day she would have to be part of the court with an old man as her husband. Never alone, representing a hundred-year-old name, entrusted to her by her father. It finally fully settled in her, that this was the reality she was living in at that moment.

She walked over to the bed, took off her shoes and in a very ungracious manner threw her head on the pillow. After the long night in the bumpy carriage this was almost as nice a feeling as the loosened corset. Although not quite.

And as fast as she had closed her eyes, as fast the world around her slipped away.

She had walked down the same hall now for almost twenty minutes. That's how big this place was. Her feet were starting to hurt in the stiff shoes and the new dress with the corset suffocated her as she tried to stand strong.

Lilly and the two other maids had woken her up exactly half an hour after she fell asleep, like she had asked, but damn if she didn't regret that decision now. She felt more tired than before and simply wished to go back to sleep, but that wouldn't be very sufficient. She had to know her way around the palace, so she knew where to go at specific times. She had wandered through the ball room, dining room, around on the second floor, through giant halls and had now made her way to a long corridor maybe leading to the front entrance.

But in reality, she was probably just lost.

To the right were windows looking out over one of the giant walls surrounding the palace. There was also a small forest area in front of it, but nothing to write home about. She could spot the amphitheater she had heard of earlier, and she could see people running around, preparing for the night's show. Under the windows were couches worked into the main construction and made cute little places to rest, which was exactly what she did.

Aimee sat down on the blue cushions, waiting for someone to pass by so she could ask for directions. She waited for what felt like hours, but finally she heard footsteps down the hall. She quickly stood up and went to meet the stranger that could help her get out of the maze.

When he got a little closer, she could begin to make out key features.

It was a young man, not much older than herself. He had a masculine figure, tall with broad shoulders, and his facial features were strong and defined, with a sturdy nose and chiseled chin. . He had long dark brown hair, and a set of warm blue eyes. They looked very familiar to her, but she couldn't remember where she had seen them before. A small scar dragged down on the side of his left eye, and for some reason he was extremely sweaty and looked like he had been in a fight.

It was also clear to her that he had forgotten to shave that morning. He wasn't wearing anything special. Just a white undone ruffle shirt, black pants, and dusty boots. By his side, he had a simple decorated sword. A single emerald was engraved on the tip of the handle.

He looked like he was thinking about something important, and the serious façade made her shiver a little. The man was actually quite handsome the closer she looked. But she ignored that fact and kept going.

"Excuse me?" she said softly, startling the man who appeared to be deeper in thought, than she had expected. He probably hadn't even seen her. The man suddenly stopped dead in his tracks, as they locked eyes and a shocked, somewhat disbelieving expression appeared on his pretty face.

"Hello. I'm sorry, but it appears I've lost my way." She laughed slightly as if it was a completely normal occurrence. "Is there any chance you would know the way to the main hall?"

She finally stopped in front of him, with the purple skirt falling nicely around her legs. Her maids had insisted she changed into a more traditional dress, with long sleeves and a black trim. Simple, but very comfortable.

The man looked at her, still somewhat shocked and confused. "It's uhm-down there," he said and pointed to a door half hidden behind a vase of flowers, "through there turn left, and then you should be able to see the main doors at the end of the hallway."

Aimee felt her face light up. "Oh, thank you so much, I feel like I've been walking around for hours. And I haven't seen a single soul to ask." She smiled at the man and a slight red tint spread across his face. "I'll be on my way now, please excuse me." Aimee bowed slightly in a goodbye and started walking toward the door.

"Wait."

She turned around in surprise and saw him standing with a hand reached out as if he was trying to grab out after her.

"Yes?" she asked in a calm demeanor, finding his awkwardness both amusing and adorable.

His expression hardened and he stood up straight.

"You look familiar... Could I have your name, please?" he asked. Aimee could see that he was trying to act tough but was fighting the natural shyness that had planted itself on his face.

She thought about it for a moment.

"A name for a name," she said calmly. "I'll tell you mine, and you'll tell me yours. Only seems fair."

A smile spread on his face.

"*Hmmm*... Very well. Please... Ladies first." he said in a mischievous tone.

"Oh, so you're also a gentleman," she remarked and a proud expression washed over him. "My name is Aimee Achillea of the Edenran Duchy. I am here attending His Highness's masquerade tomorrow."

Confusion replaced the pride on his face.

"Are you here alone? A lady of your standard is rare to see on her own, isn't she?" he asked with a raised eyebrow.

"Now that is rather personal, and I don't remember that question being part of our agreement, now was it? Your name, sir," she laughed.

Again, with the smile. He had two small dimples on each cheek. A small detail that went a long way to make him look even more handsome.

He bowed down in an exaggerated gesture and when he stood up the smile had more than doubled. "Well, my Lady, the name you're looking for is Sir Chilian. And I am at your utmost service if you were to ever get lost within the palace walls again." he grinned. Aimee raised a skeptic eyebrow.

"Oh really? No last name given?"

"I fear you might be overwhelmed by my many prestigious titles if I were to tell you."

"Ah yes, of course," Aimee said, "but what if I was in need of another rescue, and I didn't know my savior's last name? Then what would I do? Then who would I yell out too? There could be many named Chilian."

He looked at the roof while looking comically thoughtful. "Yes, well that *is* a predicament. But I can't just give my name like that to every maiden in distress. I'm afraid you would have to earn it." He shrugged his shoulders indicating his own disappointment.

"All right then. What should I do to get it?" she asked without a second thought.

He looked back at her with a devilish grin, as if she had fallen directly into his meticulous trap. "How about a dance tomorrow at the ball?"

She paused. Was it really worth it? What if he turned out to be nothing but a knight or a lowly baron's son? An unmarried, young noblewoman dancing with a knight was a scandal in itself. An embarrassment. Her father would disown her on the spot if he were to find out.

But he seemed so sure of himself and his so-called titles. The thought of him being anything less than what he played up to be, felt like mindless paranoia. And for the first time in years she was talking to someone she could laugh with. He engaged with her, he talked to her as her equal. She had always been either the highly born noble, people were bound to bow to, or the unwanted daughter of an Archduke, who was despised for existing and pushed aside in favor of her older sister.

Only if it was just for a minute, she felt heard. She felt seen. So, she took the risk.

"All right. You have a deal."

The grin briefly changed to a genuine smile but returned again quickly.

"See you there then." He turned away and started walking away down the long corridor.

"Hey wait! You said you would give me your name." Aimee yelled after him.

"Find me tomorrow! Blue mask, black suit. I'll be by the main entrance at ten. Then you'll have a name to remember!" Chilian turned around to deliver one last annoying smile and then started walking again.

Aimee was stunned. She had never had such a conversation. And then he just walked away, like nothing had happened. She would be lying if she said she wasn't intrigued.

She took a last glance at the man, before walking over to the door behind the vase. And as Chilian said, she could see the main doors down the corridor.

*

So, it was her. His Blossom.

He hadn't just imagined the comparison. Aimee was there, in the palace. She looked so different. He did too. Maybe that was why she didn't recognize him. But no matter what, his promise still stood. And it would, till the end of his days.

Chapter 3

A Dance with a Friend and a Foe

The dress was a beautiful marine green. The neckline hung low, and the sleeves were like ghosts floating around her arms, almost see-through. The skirt started right under her belly button and fell down into multiple layers of the same light kind of fabric as the sleeves. It shifted from green to a dark royal blue and a cape reaching the floor hung from Aimee's shoulders. It was attached to her wrists so it could move with her movements, making her look like a moving sea.

The mask was also wonderful. One half was green while the other was blue. Small white pearls were sewn to each side of it and to match it, her maids had picked out a pretty pearl necklace and small earrings for her to wear. Even her hair had received the small, white highlights with hairpins pinning down a small bun on the back of her hair. The rest of the red locks were slightly curled and laid comfortable on her shoulders.

The three girls should be rewarded generously the next morning. She would make sure of it.

She felt lighter than the air around her, walking through the long hallway leading to the ballroom. Already from afar she could hear the music playing. It sounded like slow piano and violins.

When she entered the giant ballroom she was stunned by all the people there. She recognized some of them, of course, due to her extensive education and the chore of remembering all the names, faces and ranks. But she had never been in a room with all of the nobles at once.

She stepped to the right of the main entrance, but when she looked at the clock there were still thirty minutes till the agreed meeting time. So meanwhile, she decided to move along the wall until she reached the snacks. As she took a glass of champagne, her eyes glanced over the assembly. Earls, viscounts, and a ton of barons. With them were all the countesses, viscountesses, and the baronesses of course, their children and their parents, and an army of servants, meeting their every demand. Many of them were all recognizable even with their masks, covering their faces.

People like the ones who had visited their estate in Leirath her entire life, and people she had read off in her many books during her tutoring. Many resembled portraits she had seen before, and she even recognized some from a garden party her father had held once.

The other Archdukes were also present. Her father, and the Archduke of Oldea, Maulus Aquil, her future brother-in-law, wasn't present. It was the Grand Duke Aman Shanlor of the Oldea duchy, surprisingly, who had come as a representative of the Aquil family. But Archduke Renan Malvaria of Stillgate was standing with his wife princess Difis Malvaria, over by the orchestra. The widow Archduchess Sonor Dahlian was also present with what looked like her two sons and young daughter. After her husband passed, she had taken over the responsibilities of the Cateron duchy. She carried her grief well and looked good for her age.

Aimee had seen those three powerhouses, Malvaria, Shanlor and Dahlian before, because they had been for dinner with her father multiple times. All nice people, but very serious. Aimee quietly wondered what her father and Archduke Aquil was doing that was so important that they couldn't be there tonight.

Suddenly, she found the fifth Archduke, the great King Aldrick Istatis in between the crowd. He was wearing a blue and golden suit with a matching mask. His almost white hair and well-kept beard was, of course, eye-catching, and Aimee wondered how she hadn't seen him before now. By his side was his daughter Princess Sofeel. She was almost the spitting image of him, just smaller, younger, and of course with more feminine features. She looked lovely in a royal blue gown, and a golden cape, draped over her shoulders. And the recognizable white hair was set up perfectly in a bun.

The princess waved to a beautiful dark-skinned woman from across the room and ran off leaving the king behind. Thankfully another, older woman came up to him and took his arm. Queen Alryn she assumed, but it was hard seeing it through the crowd of people and masks.

She couldn't seem to find the last part of the Istatis family. The party's host and her next king. Prince Maxim wasn't even at his own party. *How strange*, she thought. She believed that he was some kind of party animal, spending all the country's money on a new party every other week, just to be the center of attention. But there wasn't a trace of him anywhere.

The dance floor was packed with shiny dresses, jewelry blinding the eyes of onlookers and all sorts of different suits and costumes. It was so confusing to look at. She had been to small local balls before, but this was truly on an entirely different scale.

Without Aimee having realized the clock was already pointing at ten. *How did the time fly by so fast?*, she thought silently.

She sat down her glass and walked toward the main doors.

Luckily, the space had almost cleared up with everyone inside, and just as the mystery man had promised, there he was.

Chilian was in a handsome black suit, a dark blue cape covering half of his broad shoulders and a mask in a shady blue covered his face. She could still see the warm eyes under it, and that, for some reason, made her stomach act up a little. The dark brown hair was no longer messy like the night before, but brushed back with a tiny strand having escaped the wax, now hanging in front of his forehead.

He was even more handsome than at their first meeting, which her brain had trouble fully understanding.

"I thought you had forgotten all about me," Chilian said in a calm but jokingtone. He gently took Aimee's hand in his and placed a light kiss on the back of it. A small wave of heat rushed from her hand to the rest of her body in less than a second, but she remained calm.

"I would never," she said, "we do have a deal, don't we, Mr. Mystery?"

"Oh no. I thought you would have forgotten about that by now. That's why I took so long getting ready." He laughed in a teasing tone and gestured to his new look.

"Your name, or I'm leaving right here and now." Aimee said with a smile and turned around to walk away.

"No, no, no, no, please don't go." Chilian gently grabbed her wrist and she stopped. She slowly turned back around to look at him, surprised by his sudden soft tone.

He sighed.

"Chilian Malvaria. Of the Stillgate Duchy. Happy?" He looked at her. His grip tightening around her wrist.

Her eyes were wide open. It was like her throat was tied together and she couldn't breathe as she realized who she was facing.

"You're the son of Renan Malvaria... Heir to Stillgate and second to the throne!" She bowed her head down as far as possible to try and hide the embarrassment on her face. "I deeply apologize for the way I acted, I wasn't aware that you were the king's nephew. If I had known I would have never—" she didn't get to finish her rambling before she felt two firm hands on her shoulders.

"Stop, stop, stop... Please."His eyes met hers, and it was like sorrow had spread across them, like a heavy veil. "Don't treat me any differently. You're one of the only people I've ever had a conversation with without feeling alienated. Please just think of me as Chilian. Your friendly knight." He finished with a tired smile.

He was still holding onto her, his grip tightening slightly, waiting for an answer. He looked desperate and she felt his pain. Being viewed as an untouchable political figure her entire life, she could understand him to a certain degree. She stared at him still in a somewhat state of shock, but realized that she was only torturing him further by not saying anything. So she took a deep breath, and laid her hand on his, still resting on her shoulders.

"Is this why you wouldn't tell me?" A soft smile grew on her lips, and she could see the worry on his face lifting slightly.

"I guess, you could say that." He took her hand and held it in his own, gentler than she would have imagined. They were rough, probably from sword fighting or some other sport, but still well maintained. He looked like someone who would join the soldiers on the training grounds if given the chance. She liked that about him.

She had never smiled at him like that.

It was reassuring. And loving. He had only ever gotten that smile from his mother. Chilian's breath was almost sucked away by it. It was now he actually realized how beautiful she looked. The dress was a good contrast to her dark pink hair, and the pearls only highlighted her features even more. He had never been much for jewelry, thinking it was a waste of money, but on her, it was so simple and yet so defining it made it all worth it. He wanted to thank whoever got them for her. Personally.

He took Aimee's hand and held it in midair. "By the way... You look beautiful tonight." He sent her a small cocky smile to lighten the mood again, and she looked more flustered than ever before. She was entirely red under the green and blue mask and her mouth was trying to form some kind of thanks, but it just came out as a muttering blur.

He couldn't help but laugh teasingly at her struggle, which only earned him a deadly stare. "Well. I think you promised a dance, am I right, m'Lady?" It was like she snapped back to reality, and suddenly looked part determined, and part, more confused than a chicken running wild.

"Y-Yeah I did. Please lead the way," she said. And so he did. He took her hand and laid it over his arm and like that they walked out to the dance floor. They waited for a spot to open up and glided smoothly into the next music number. They swayed back and forth and spun around following the crowd and the musical flow. All of the steps were perfect as all the nobles had received extensive dance lessons. It was a required skill for getting entry to these kinds of events.

But he had to admit that she was more elegant and precise in her movements than any dance teacher he had ever met. She moved with such grace and beauty that he was completely entranced by her. He had rarely experienced that with anyone else before. He was speechless.

The music changed to a calm waltz, and they slowly swayed across the floor.

"What's wrong, kind sir? You're suddenly so awfully silent. Did you use up all of your jokes already?" Aimee asked while staring out over the crowd of nobles. She turned around and looked at him with those turquoise eyes of hers and with a smirk plastered on her lips.

"No, no. I was just simply enjoying the view from up here." He wasn't kidding as he was a head taller than her and truly enjoyed looking down on her from the height. She looked adorable in his big arms, and at the same time extremely fragile. Like a single rough movement would break her in half. Like a porcelain doll.

Aimee gave him an annoyed look, but quickly moved on.

"So, you're king Aldrick's nephew?" she asked.

"Yeah. On my mother's side."

"His sister, right?"

"Correct."

"So how come when we met in the hallway you looked like a commoner on his way back from a street fight?" she asked bluntly. It took him by surprise but he answered shortly after.

"First of all, I wasn't that beat up, how rude of you. Second of all, I was a simple knight on his way back from training." Aimee turned her head back to look at him, confused by his answer. *Cute,* he thought to himself. "I train with the kings' guards every other day. It started out as plain entertainment for them, teaching a young noble the way of the sword, but as I kept coming it became routine. Now I'm a part time trainer for the younger men and I was knighted two years back," Chilian said.

"Really?" Aimee sounded naturally curious.

"Yeah. It was a distraction method. Life in the palace can become quite boring, so it was a great place to escape it all and let out some of the frustration. What about you? Do you have a place like that?" They made eye contact and he was surprised to see them sadden a little. She looked away and Chilian feared that he might have made a mistake, asking such a personal question.

A moment passed by.

"You don't need to answer."

"But I do, don't I?" she said, while glaring out into the crowd. "A small pond, in the gardens of my home. I found it when I was little and only I and a few others know about it. It's a nice place to escape to."

Chilian's heart skipped a beat. *She still came there?*

She stopped dancing, and just stared down at the floor. Chilian once again took her hand. He held it up to his mouth and kissed the back of it, like a true gentleman. "Do me a favor and take me there sometime. Thank you for the dance," he said.

A sad smile rested on her face, and he felt awful for making her feel that way. "Wanna get something to drink?" he asked, and she nodded hesitantly.

As they left the dancefloor he couldn't help, but wondering why the mentioning of the pond had made her so sad. All the joy had drained from her face leaving only an empty expression, reminiscent of the lifeless portraits hanging throughout the castle.

Perhaps she did remember? He felt a small flame light inside of him as it could be a possibility. He couldn't stop a small smile from forming on his lips.

They went to the snack table and each found a glass of some kind of alcohol. The banter quickly resumed and for the rest of the night they were almost inseparable. They talked and talked for what felt like hours about everything and nothing. Their thoughts on politics, all the drama going around the palace and their favorite past times. Chilian had never felt this connected to another person, and he loved every second of it.

It had gotten quite late when Aimee asked to retire for the night.

"Could I ask you a favor?" she asked him.

"Of course. Anything," he said with no hesitation.

"I'm afraid I still don't know my way to the main stairs. Would it be too much trouble for you to walk me there? It is possible, I am a little too drunk to dare and try walking there on my own." She laughed. He was surprised by the trust she was giving him, but he took Aimee under his arm and said, "Anything for you, my Lady." With a warm smile on his face. She turned red again and just like that, they were off, for the second floor.

They had a little trouble walking straight through the corridors and when they reached the stair she almost tripped over her own feet on the way up and blamed it on her dress.

*

They finally made it to her quarters, with no major incidents, and Aimee suddenly felt a heavy feeling in her stomach, when she realized it was time to say goodbye.

"Thank you so much for tonight," she said, "I had feared I would have been confined to the sidelines, simply watching everyone else having a good time."

"I should be the one thanking you, for this night. I wasn't even planning on attending, but the thought of dancing with you was too irresistible." he said with a smug smile.

"That's a bit cheesy, isn't it?" she asked with a laugh.

"You tell me."

Aimee looked up at Chilian with a curious expression. Never in her life had she met someone so blunt, funny and charming all at once. She enjoyed being with him and wished for him to just stay by her side.

"Thank you." she said again and opened the door to her chambers.

"W-Wait."

Aimee turned around immediately, trying to hide her smile and excitement. "Yes?"

She could see him fidgeting with his hand, clearly nervous about what he was about to say.

"Would it be possible to see you tomorrow? Before you leave the palace, that is?"

He sounded so sincere. The shyness of a young boy shined through his confident exterior and she couldn't help but feel her knees weaken a little under her. She said, "Yes."

He lit up. "Then could you meet me in the gardens then. At twelve?" he asked.

She nodded with a giant smile.

Aimee reached up into her hair and pulled out the main pearl- hairpin that kept everything together. The dark pink curls fell down over her shoulders and tickled her skin, sending goosebumps up her arms. Then she gave him the hairpin.

"Deliver it back tomorrow. I'll be waiting by the center fountain. Don't disappoint me." Aimee said with an almost whisper. He looked at the hairpin with big eyes and turned to her with a smile. He led the pearl to his lips and kissed it gently.

"Tomorrow then," he said with a laugh, and she couldn't help but laugh along with him.

"Goodnight, Chilian Malvaria." She closed the door and waited on the other side.

When she heard his footsteps walk away, it felt like an entire swarm of butterflies was released in her stomach.

But when she turned around, however, her three maids stood and stared at her with round eyes. She hadn't even noticed them standing ready with both tea and a few biscuits on a platter, simply listening to their conversation.

"It is not what it sounds like," she said, trying to convince them that it wasn't what they all clearly witnessed. She damned her bright, burning cheeks and nervous behavior.

Lilly stood with her arms crossed and a raised eyebrow. "M'Lady, it sounded like you are going on a date tomorrow."

Aimee regretted giving Lilly the clear to talk to her as a friend.

"It's not like that." Aimee tried, but they were already convinced. Sheldy had trouble coming back to reality after the initial shock and Linari, the youngest looking, simply looked amazed. "How romantic with the hairpin..." she mumbled underneath her breath, which earned her an elbow in the side by the other two.

Aimee buried her face in her hands in embarrassment. She felt Lilly's trusty hand on her shoulder. "Don't worry, Lady Aimee. We'll make sure you look your absolute best tomorrow."

She felt a smile forming over the knowledge that she had someone rooting for her.

Setting the nerves and burning cheeks aside she was happy.

She was so thankful for that evening. For the first time ever she felt her father's decision had made a positive impact on her life.

For the first time in a long time she was happy and excited for the next day to come.

She couldn't sleep. She was maybe too excited. She tossed and turned but no matter what she did, she just couldn't keep her eyes shut. So she decided to go for a walk in the gardens. It was about one in the night, but the party was still going strong when she passed by. Now, however, it just sounded like a lot of drunk idiots yelling over the music.

The gardens were quiet though. It was a bit cold so Aimee had brought a thick shawl she had found in her closet. Her night gown was very thin, but still good enough to be passed off as an old-fashioned day-to-day dress, with a high waist and lots of lace. She had a pair of shoes with a small heel, and her hair hung loose, so everytime she took a step on the paths she felt a slight tickle around her neck.

The gardens were dimly lit by the moon, and it gave the mighty garden an eerie feeling. But, nonetheless, the air was clear and so was the sky. The further away from the palace she came, the more stars she could see. They were all beautiful and in different colors. *Incredible,* she thought to herself.

She kept walking down the stone path until she reached the trees that resembled a small forest. The path branched off in two different ways. She looked around, and saw the guards lined up along the walls of the palace keeping a close eye on her. She wanted to be alone however, so she went down the path leading to the forest. The long road became smaller and smaller, until it rounded out in a small open field with trees all around her. There, on the other side of the clearing was an overgrown wall with an old door that seemed awfully random. She grabbed a hold of the small golden handle and turned it slowly.

The door creaked open and revealed a small magical garden.

Trees still surrounded her, but there was also a small pond. It was a bit green with algae covering the water, but it was there.

The moon made it all look blue and comforting. A bench was placed on the other side of the pond and just like her hideout, there were lanterns hanging down from the branches. They weren't lit though.

She was in awe.

It was almost exactly like her own pond back at home.

She went over to sit down on the bench. In the distance she heard an owl howl and somewhere in the water a frog was quacking. She imagined the duck and her ducklings swimming around, and a small smile managed its way onto her face.

She felt at peace there in the moonlight, surrounded by trees and nature, so she closed her eyes and let the time go by.

She felt her mind settle down and the excitement vanish as her breathing slowed. From the two days she had spent in the palace she had felt the extreme stress that can come with a life in luxury. People yelling and drinking, servants everywhere waiting for your demands, and the constant need for elegance and class. It was hell sometimes.

So here in between the trees where there was silence and peace she allowed herself to let down her guard.

"What's this? An intruder…"

Aimee jumped in fright and frantically looked to where the voice was coming from.

In the dark stood a tall man, with white hair and clothes in blue and gold.

He was looking directly at her, and a relaxed smug was resting on his face. A cape was attached to his shoulders and a decorated sword with lapis lazuli covering the handle was resting by his hip. On his blue jacket a number of medals was hanging in four rows and Aimee wondered how she hadn't heard him coming through the door with all that clinging metal. He didn't look much older than herself.

But it was his eyes. Beautiful blue sapphire stones, except that they were organic and not crystals. They reminded her of Chilian's. But they weren't warm or kind. Or comforting. These eyes were hard. Decisive and cold. Hateful even.

Aimee stood up quickly and bowed down. "Sir, I apologize. I didn't know this place was private. I'll take my leave immediately."

"Sir? That's a first," the stranger said. Aimee lifted her head and saw the man smirking at her menacingly.

"Excuse me…" she said and started walking toward the door with a lowered head. But when she tried to go through it, the man didn't move. "Sir, if you would be so kind as to move—"

She barely finished her sentence before the stranger grabbed a painful hold of her jaw with one hand and held her arms behind her with the other. Aimee gasped in surprise and tried fighting against him, but without luck.

"Never in my life," he said slowly, "has anyone dared to call me anything but his Highness. Now." The man pulled her face closer to his own. "What do you think, gives you the right to call me something so lowly, as sir?" he asked in a cold tone.

Aimee continued to struggle, but his grip only tightened. "I don't know who you are!" she managed to get out through the pain under his fingers.

The man's eyes widened, and the smile shortly faded. But it returned even wider than before, seemingly finding her dimwittedness entertaining.

"Please let go of me! I have done nothing wrong!" she pleaded, while feeling the tears pushing alarmingly on her eyes.

He looked her up and down, his expression not changing a bit. Then he looked at her directly. "If you try and think, *really* think, would you recognize me?" He asked menacingly. Aimee's head tossed and turned, trying to figure out if she had ever seen him before. The only one she could think of immediately was the blue eyed boy in the painting. That could be her only chance of making it out of the situation.

"P-Prince Maxim…?" she mumbled through the still increasing pain in her jar. He was quiet for a second, and she couldn't read his expression. Then his grip loosened, and Aimee fell trembling to the ground, gasping for air.

Though she froze completely when she felt a hand running through her hair.

"This is a rare color…" the prince said. "Tell me. What is your name? And why is a young lady like you walking around in the night, in nothing but a shawl and a nightgown?" he asked.

She dared not look at him. "My name is Aimee Achillea, of the Edenran Duchy… I was out for fresh air," she said, her voice shakier than before. She hated how petrified she felt.

"Ahh. I thought you looked familiar. You're Sir Erlan's daughter. The youngest one, am I right?" She nodded hesitantly. "*Hmmm*. How curious." He gently placed his fingers under her chin and forced her to look up at him. The touch made her sick and she wanted to more or less punch him in his smirking face. He examined her extensively and when he was done he went quiet for a long while.

"A shame with those marks on your pretty jaw," he simply said, "make sure to cover them up if they aren't gone by tomorrow—" he paused for a while. Staring at her. "…I like you…" he said coldly and stood up, "However you have trespassed in the crown prince's private gardens. For this you shall be punished. I will make sure it happens. Run along now." He stood up and started walking over to the other side of the pond where he sat down on the bench.

"Yo-Your highness," Aimee mustered up, under the fear. "What punishment?"

He looked dead at her, like a hawk staring at its prey. Sizing her up.

"*Hmmm*... I don't know yet. Not something very pleasant I presume." He looked at the sky. "You could get out of this whole situation if you promptly apologized and maybe, begged on your knees for my forgiveness... There's no guarantee though."

Aimee looked at him with nothing but disgust. But she hesitantly stood up from the ground and tried to put one of her many calm facades on.

"I apologize deeply for trespassing on your land," she said in a still pretty shaken voice. For some stupid reason she felt awfully brave in that one moment and didn't want to show him the satisfaction he desired. "I will, however, not beg on the ground for anyone's forgiveness. That is below me."

The same second the last word had left her, she regretted ever opening mouth. But she couldn't go back now. She had no choice, but to continue.

Prince Maxim was surprisingly not furious. Instead, he looked amazed by her audacity to talk to him in such a way. "You're playing with something you don't want to, little doll. Are you sure you wanna continue like that?" he asked, still with the fascinated smile on his face.

She couldn't back down now. She had just challenged the crown prince and all of his power. This was going to have some kind of consequences, she knew it, but her body told her to just walk away. If it was her pride or her fear that wanted to run she didn't know, but she had no other choice.

"I am certain." And then she did the most reckless thing she had done all her life. "Goodnight, your Highness."

She bowed down and turned around. And then she walked away without permission. She almost ran, trying to get as far away from that pond as possible, before the tears started flowing.

Chapter 4

Flower Crowns and Buns

Prince Maxim had been right in regards to the marks on her jaw, as she looked into the mirror.

Where his fingers had been, there were now big red prints covering her from the lower chin down to her neck.

It still hurt.

The door to the bedroom suddenly opened up and in came Linari. Usually at this time, Lilly would have brought her breakfast, but strangely Linari only carried a teapot on a small platter with milk, sugar cubes, and a cup.

She gently placed the beverage on Aimee's dining table and was about to take her leave.

"Wait. Where's my breakfast?" Aimee asked in confusion and left the mirror to study this weird arrangement.

"The crown prince's orders," she said in a timid voice. Linari reached into her pocket and took out a small piece of paper. Aimee snatched it from her hand and frantically opened the note.

Miss Aimee Achillea is not to be allowed any food until I say otherwise.

She is only to have beverages accompanied with either sugar, or ice cubes, of her own liking.

- Prince Maxim Istatis.

The son of a bitch was going to starve her…

She looked at the note with a bitter taste in her mouth. Linari was still standing, waiting anxiously for her reaction.

In truth she felt powerless. Like a giant rug was pulled from under her feet, and she was now tumbling through a dark pit.

"Thank you… You can leave…" Amiee mumbled.

"Of course, my Lady," Linari said, and in the next second she was gone, out of the door.

Aimee stared at the note. It felt like it was burning up her hand. Then she promptly crumbled it into a ball and let it fall to the ground. She had never gone without food for a longer period, so this was going to be pure torture. She had what? Two days left in the palace?

And the worst thing was that she had a meeting with Chilian later that day. How could she look anybody in the eyes after such embarrassment? She thought about canceling, but that would only make it suspicious. And she didn't want to cancel. She didn't want to disappoint him.

So, she decided to go.

Her maids picked out a nice simple dress with a collar, covering most of her neck. She was relieved when none of them asked about the marks. The dress was a dark red color and was made with a heavy material weighing down on her shoulders. The skirt fell in waves behind her, and the corset sat loose under the long-sleeved bodice.

They let her slightly curly hair hang loose but attached a small pearl comb on the side of her head. And lastly, a very cheap looking necklace with a single pearl attached in the middle, brought the entire outfit together.

Extremely simple and almost seamless in the sea of gold and crystal jewelry walking around out in the palace's halls.

And like that, she was ready.

*

Aimee was ten minutes late.

Chilian had arrived at the center fountain, like she had asked him, but she was nowhere to be found.

He feared something had happened to her, or maybe she had forgotten? But he reasoned that she had just overslept. She did seem a bit tipsy the night before, so it wouldn't surprise him. He reached down to his pocket and pulled out the small hairpin. He was mesmerized by it. That small pearl hair piece was proof of their conversation last night, and her promise to come and pick it up again today. That was his ticket.

The garden looked beautiful today.

The grass was green and fresh, all the flowers were colorful, and the sun was shimmering in a cloudless sky. The perfect day for such an occasion.

"Sir Chilian!" He turned around in a heartbeat and saw Aimee almost running out the palace's glass doors. He automatically started walking toward her and they met in the middle. A tired face met his, when she looked up at him, and immediately he noticed the black circles under her eyes, despite her maids' attempts of covering them.

"Did you have a little too much to drink last night or are you always this fatigued in the morning?" He laughed and a tired smile spread on her lips.

"Just a bad night's sleep, that's all," she answered calmly.

"Oh really? Did the thought of me keep you up all night, my Lady?" She turned bright red and instinctively turned to look at the ground. Bingo.

"You look beautiful today. As always. I especially love your jewelry. Does it have any particular meaning or is it just to make your remarkable smile stand out?" he asked flirtingly. She looked up at him, with an embarrassed expression, and she was even more adorable than normal. But he didn't tell her that.

She took a small breath, and a serious smile found its way to her lips.

"Oh, so you noticed. It's because I'm awaiting a gift from a certain someone, and I thought I would take it into use immediately. So I found something to match."

He raised an eyebrow.

"And what certain someone is the young lady perhaps talking about?"

"*Hmmm...* A knight, you could say."

"A knight?" She nodded. "Isn't that a bit of a scandal? A noble woman and a simple knight? How would her family react to such embarrassment?" He made a worried face and was happy to see her face lighting up.

"I guess, we'll have to keep it a secret for now..." she said in a somber voice. To her credit she was a really good actor.

A gentle smile sneaked its way onto his face, and he took a step forward. They were almost closer than the night before, where they had danced together. He reached down and grabbed her hand. With the other still holding the hairpin, he placed the piece in her hair, next to the comb she already had in place.

Then he leaned in over her and kissed the pearls white surface a last time, before looking down at Aimee again. He was still holding her hand and the distance between them was smaller than ever.

Her eyes were wide, and her cheeks ruby red.

His Blossom. She had changed a lot since back then. For the

better.

But she didn't remember him. She didn't recognize him. She had completely forgotten all about that summer, all those years ago. And no matter how long he had tossed and turned last night, he couldn't figure out why.

A heavy feeling wrapped around his chest, and it became hard to breathe as he stared down into those familiar eyes.

*

Aimee could see the sadness spreading on Chilian's face. His grip around her hand tightened and she felt her flustered expression turn serious. She gently lifted her hand up to his face and placed it on his cheek.

"What's wrong…?" she asked in a quiet voice. He almost jumped at the touch of her fingers, and his sad expression quickly changed.

"Nothing, I just remembered something. Where would you like to go?" he asked, once again sounding playful and witty. She stared at him for a little while before she realized that her hand was still resting on his cheek.

Embarrassed, she quickly pulled away from him and laid down the proper distance between a young man and woman. *How disgraceful,* she thought. They had only just met, and yet they were so intimate. The only person she should be that close with was a future husband, and she didn't look forward to that.

She looked around for a bit.

"How about going to the flower field?" she asked. "They're beautiful, even from here, but I wanna see them up close."

Chilian looked at her warmly. "Well, if that's what the Lady wants, that's what the Lady is going to get."

"Please, just call me Aimee. The formality drives me crazy," she said.

"Only if you stop calling me sir," he answered back. "It makes me feel like an old man." He reached out his arm and she placed her own under it. And like that they were off.

The pair had walked for a while when a thought popped into her head.

"I wanted to ask you," she started, "you're the crown princes' cousin, am I right?"

He nodded. "Yes, why?"

"Does your cousin seem... I don't know. Off, to you in any way?"

Chilian's glare stiffened, and he turned to look warily at her. He quickly looked around to see if anyone could hear them, but they were all alone, and out of range from the guards lining the walls.

"My cousin has never had a completely clear mind. He is probably paranoid about his delegate position as the heir, and it may have gotten to him. Since he was a child, there has been something wrong with him. He abused cats and worked his nannies to death. He has gotten better since then, but I would advise you to steer clear of him."

Steer clear of him, yeah good job there Aimee.

He paused for a bit. "Why do you ask about him?"

She thought about it for a moment.

"I had the pleasure of running into him yesterday."

Chilian stopped dead in his tracks and turned toward her. His face looked pale, and he had a somewhat frightened expression. Aimee had clearly made a mistake mentioning Prince Maxim, so she quickly tried to brush it off. "It wasn't anything special! We just exchanged a few words and then he was off to who knows where." She nervously laughed in the hope he wouldn't question it further, but his expression barely changed.

"If you say so…" Chilian mumbled, mostly to himself, but Aimee could hear the worry in his voice, and it gave her a warm feeling inside.

They finally reached the flower field. It was a well-organized sea of all kinds of flowers in all imaginable colors. She let go of Chilian's arm and almost ran the last bit towards the sea of beautiful colors. A slight breeze flew over them, making all the flowers dance, and it was almost like she was back in her own garden.

When she was younger she used to spend almost every single day out there, simply admiring their pretty colors and patterns. She always spent hours, trying to count all the different shades or individual flowers of a specific species.

The achillea flowers had always been her favorite, for obvious reasons. When she was small she was convinced the flower was named after her family, but she luckily grew smarter with age.

Sometimes she would make a small bouquet representing her family. A small, dark pink achillea for her. A light yellow, almost beige for her father. A smaller and similar flower for her older sister Elniba. And a slightly bigger pink, one for her mother. For her nanny she always found a pretty white one, and for some variation she also picked up a dark blue flower too.

The first time she had done this she wanted to show it to her father. But instead of him being proud of her he simply got angry and told her to Get out of his office. Simple gestures like that always angered him, so she learned quickly that she had no chance of winning him over with that sort of thing.

Her nanny had felt sorry for her and one day a book, with all kinds of flower species, had been placed on her bedside table.

She loved that book.

"Anything interesting in today's batch?" Chilian knelt down beside her and started digging around in the many thick, and luscious petals.

"I've almost always had a fascination with flowers," she said with a broad smile. "They just always made me so happy."

Chilian mumbled something to himself, too quiet to hear, so Aimee brushed it off. "This might seem like a stupid question. But what's your favorite color?"

Chilian let out a light laugh, still looking at the many flowers. "What are we, ten?"

"What? It's a good question that says a lot about people's personality," she said, trying to defend her stupid question. But it was difficult keeping a straight face.

"Well, what if I was to say, that it was blue? What would that say about me?" Chilian sat down on the path next to her, with his legs stretch out and his arms supporting his weight behind his back.

He looked relaxed.

"*Hmmm.*" Aimee sat down on her knees next to him. "I'm not sure, but I think I read somewhere that people with a preference for blue are very easy going, and values friendship." She looked over at Chilian and his expression was so warm and happy, she was almost taken aback.

"And what might the young lady's favorite color be?" he asked.

"Oh no, no, no," she answered, "I don't believe I've gotten a proper answer from you. Your answer was only hypothetical."

He smiled at her. In a quick movement he sat up, crossed his legs and rested his arms on his knees.

"Well..." he said in defeat. He looked at the sky for a moment to think. It was a nice sunny weather, and while he was thinking Aimee was beginning to regret the dress with the thick material in the hot sun. "I think turquoise," he finally said. "What does that say about me?"

"That's a unique color. I don't think I remember..." she said doubtfully.

"Aw, please," he jokingly begged, "It's the only thing I've ever wanted to know." He sounded overly desperate, and it made Aimee laugh out loud. Chilian joined her quickly and there they were, on the ground, laughing at colors.

It felt so familiar and nice, just being herself around him.

"I think I know, although it might be wrong." She laughed out trying to catch her breath.

"Well, tell me!" Chilian said impatiently.

"I think turquoise has something to do with being easy going and sincere."

"Are you sure about that?"

"What? You think I'm wrong?" Aimee asked, the smile still strongly present.

"It's not that I think it's wrong." Chilian laid down on the small patch of grass between the path and the flowers, with his arms behind his head, like nothing in the world could bother him. "I just don't really see myself as especially sincere." He closed both his eyes and just seemed to enjoy the warmth of the sun on his skin.

"Well, it's just a color," Aimee responded and once again focused her attention on the flowers. "You know it's not proper for a gentleman to lie down on the ground like that."

"And it's not proper for a Lady to dirty her dress, next to a gentleman laying down, right? Court etiquette, for eight-year old's."

"I think I can bend the rules a little," she said.

"Well then so can I, don't you think?" he chuckled. And she shook her head with a big smile over the dumb conversation.

A break let the atmosphere settle, and the calmness of the scenery really started to set in.

"So, what's your favorite color?" he asked.

"Light blue."

"*Hm*." Chilian sat up, halfway leaning on his arms, and looked at her. He reached into his pocket and pulled out a small purple box. "Guess I got the wrong color then." He laughed to himself, and gently placed the box in her hand. She stared at it in shock.

"Chilian, you didn't have to get me anything, it's just a walk in the garden."

"Just opened it already. I've been waiting all day and I am going to scream if I don't see your reaction soon." He gave her a teasing smile and she couldn't help but roll her eyes at him.

She opened the small box and inside was a pair of beautiful dark pink earrings. It was two pretty gemstones that hung in a wrapping of silver thread making small circle-like patterns and a further two translucent gems were connected between the hook for her ear and the pink stones. She didn't know if it was diamonds or some kind of quarts. But they were lovely and most likely very precious.

"You shouldn't have done this…" she said with a tender smile. She didn't really mean it though. Nobody had ever given her a gift like this before. Her father had given her jewelry and a dress here and there, but that was only out of necessity. This was completely different. "When did you even get these?" she asked.

Chilian smiled and laid back down in the grass.

"After we said goodbye last night, I went straight to the royal jewelry smith. I was so mesmerized by your hair that I picked out those two garnet gems. Although now I fear that I might have made a mistake."

"Why?"

"Because they're completely unnoticeable when compared to your hair," he said in a dramatically sad voice while hiding his face of despair in his hands. Aimee couldn't help but grin at his terrible dilemma.

"They're beautiful."

She laid a gentle hand on his shoulder as a thanks. He simply nodded.

She took the earrings out of the box, and like all other jewelry, they glittered in the light. But in a different way. A better way. Because someone had thought of her and created them for her and her only. It wasn't a luxurious mass-produced product, or a rich lady's usual decoration. It was made for her and her alone. That was something she had never received.

"How long did it take to make them?" she asked while putting them on. They were a bit heavy, but very comfortable.

"All night I think," Chilian answered. "Poor jewelry smith. I woke him up, saying it was urgent, and the man probably hasn't rested since."

"You're cruel."

"And yet you're wearing them," he returned. And sadly, she couldn't do anything but agree.

She looked out over the flower field again. She wanted to return him for the earrings so she decided to make something with the only material she had at her disposal.

She worked quickly and only with the biggest ones, and in less than a few minutes, she sat with a pretty flower crown, composed of blue, white, and violet lilies and roses.

"Sit up and close your eyes," She said while hiding her masterpiece.

Chilian looked skeptical at first but obeyed and returned to the way he was sitting before, with crossed legs and closed eyes.

She placed the crown on his head and his eyes widened when he realized what it was, For a moment a hint of soft blush covered his cheeks.

She smiled and stood up, brushing off the dirt on her dress. She took a hold of her skirt and in a dramatic movement, bowed before him. "My king," she said and Chilian quickly realized what she was doing.

He was on his feet, quicker than expected, and bowed just as dramatically. "My Lady, if I'm the king then I shall have a queen, shan't I?" he asked, in a way too over the top voice.

Aimee crossed her arms and shot out her hip, in a sassy way. "Of course, you should have a queen, your highness, but I believe a simple request isn't enough for me to accept." He looked at her, not really sure of her thought process, but went along with it anyway.

"I have lands, and riches and palaces all over the kingdom. Is that not good enough for thee?" She shook her head. "If I prove myself a worthy dancer, would you then consider me a potential suitor?"

"Perhaps," she declared.

Chilian smiled devilishly, grabbed her by the waist, and they started swaying in a fast-paced waltz. They laughed their hearts out, while purposely trying to trip the other with their own feet.

It must've looked very weird from a distance, but Aimee didn't care. She was happy at that moment. She wasn't usually allowed to act in such a way and was always scolded for such behavior. Her laughter shortly died, by the thought, and for the brief second she had let her guard down, Chilian took the chance and managed to trip her feet, so she fell over. She didn't let go of his hand though, and with a hard thud they landed beside each other in the flowers.

They laughed again and Chilian clumsily got off the ground again to help her up.

"Hurry, if they see we made a mess of the flowers, I'll get stable duties for a week!" he said and lifted Aimee onto her feet. And then they started speed walking back to the palace, laughing the entire way.

They turned the volume down to a low giggling when they reached the main hall. Aimee's arm was wrapped around his, and without knowing where they were heading, Chilian led them to another long corridor, isolated from the rest of the building.

They found a long couch with blue cushions, under one of the giant windows and promptly sat down. The window was looking out over the training grounds, where people were going about their day, with training and gear inspections.

The laughter died out shortly after, and they sat in silence for a bit.

"I wanna thank you," Aimee said quietly.

"Why?" Chilian asked.

"Because I've never been able to act so freely. Even if we've only known each other a few days, I've had more fun than ever before." His smile disappeared and was replaced with a somewhat confused look. She continued, "I've never been able to be myself around others. Never been able to laugh in this way with anyone. I grew up very isolated. I was afraid of coming here, because I thought I would be isolated and the subject of rumors, as yesterday was my first real social gathering. But thanks to you

I've had the greatest time of my life. Even if it's been brief." Stupidly enough she felt a lump in her throat as she spoke, indicating that she was about to cry over a complete stranger. She felt so dumb in that moment. "So, thank you…"

Chilian looked stunned. And suddenly, it was like a black cloud rolled in over him. His expression darkened and he looked serious and saddened. "You really don't remember?" he mumbled beneath his breath.

"Remember what?"

She looked at him awaiting an answer, but he shook it off.

"You're leaving tomorrow. Right?"

It was like a kick to the stomach.

She had almost forgotten that she only had a day left at the palace. She would have to return to her home, where no one wanted her, and where everyone saw her face as a curse.

Everything froze around her. She didn't want to go back. To the isolation. She didn't want to leave that warmth she had found by Chilian's side.

But it wasn't a choice. It was her father's will that she returned. And if she stayed, the prince was probably going to keep tormenting her. Now that she thought about it, she was quite hungry…

Aimee took a deep breath and collected her thoughts.

"I don't think I want to leave…" Her voice was shaky.

It was like her words had pierced Chilian. His hands started shaking and his expression almost looked painful. Remorseful actually.

After a little while, he took her hand and brushed the back of it with his thumb.

"Believe it or not. I'm not popular with the ladies in the castle. Nor am I interested in them. But I don't want you to leave.

I don't want to be separated again."

She tilted her head. "Why do you say things like that?"

His grip around her hand tightened as she saw him tear up a little.

"You really don't remember?"

Aimee felt like one big question mark. *Did she know him from somewhere?*

They were silent until he sighed and asked, "Can I come visit you…?"

Aimee was surprised by the request, but she didn't show it. "I'm not quite sure. I don't know what my father would say to a man visiting me. I actually don't know if he would even care…" she mumbled as she thought about the many possible responses the Archduke could come with.

Aimee looked down at Chilian's hands. They were very big compared to hers. And a little rough. But also warm. She sighed and as she had done the night before, she reached up for the pin in her hair, and pulled out the pearl. She looked up at Chilian with a tender smile, and he stared from her to the accessory, confused.

"This sounds stupid, but I want you to have it. You don't have to deliver it back, or anything. I just want you to keep it… As a reminder maybe." Tears had started threatening to break loose now, but she kept everything inside.

She got free of his grip and reached up to place the hairpin somewhere it wouldn't get lost. On his collar was a good place, she decided. She quickly attached it to his formal waistcoat and she could feel Chilian's stare the entire time.

He sat quiet for a bit. Everything had felt so nice and warm, just a few moments before, and now they were both in silence, having realized that their time together probably was nothing but a small encounter that none of them would remember in a few years.

"Well, hello there. How sad you both look." Aimee stiffened as she recognized the cold, arrogant voice. Every warmth in her body disappeared as she recognized the tall figure with the white hair coming walking toward them from down the hall.

Chilian looked more annoyed than frightened and stood up to greet his cousin Prince Maxim.

"Your Highness. What a surprise to see you here," he said. Aimee didn't see the prince's expression. She stared intensively at the floor, hoping that he had forgotten all about her, and saw her as nothing more than any other noble woman in the court.

"Well, you see I was just on my way to another meeting. I was planning to stop by Lady Aimee's quarters, but I suppose that won't be necessary," Prince Maxim said, with an unnerving optimism. The fact that he was planning on stopping by her room was enough to make her sick. "but then I saw the two of you here and decided to go say hi. Now. What were you doing before I so rudely interrupted?" asked the prince.

She couldn't explain why, but she knew that he was scheming something. You could hear it in his voice. She got goosebumps.

Aimee saw Chilian's feet shift around, a bit uncomfortable. He was nervous.

"We were just talking about your masquerade yesterday. It was quite exciting if I may, but a shame that we barely saw anything to you," Chilian replied.

"I'm afraid I had some urgent business. But how nice of you." Prince Maxim went silent for a bit.

"And what about you, little doll?" Aimee completely froze. "Did you enjoy the party as well?"

She forced herself to look at him. He was smirking coldly at her. His hair had been combed back, and he had changed from the formal wear into a snowy white uniform.

His pants were light blue and the black boots from yesterday had been switched to a pair of elegant shoes.

Chilian was looking at her too, both confused and concerned. She had told him that the two of them had briefly met the night before, but the nickname was something that couldn't be explained so easily.

She was doomed.

"I agree, your Highness. It was a very delightful event," she spun in a sweet voice, hoping to hide the fear.

Prince Maxim looked at her for a moment. He turned and smiled at Chilian.

Then the prince walked straight past him and stopped right in front of Aimee. No matter how good her acting skills were, she clearly showed how frightened she was. Every cell in her body was screaming at her to run, and every muscle was trying its best to act natural.

Without warning he once again grabbed her jaw and left her no choice but to stand up, as he raised her head. She could hear Chilian scrambling like he wanted to run towards them, but ultimately didn't.

She couldn't see anything but Prince Maxim's pale face and cold blue eyes staring at her.

Prince Maxim took a long look at her, studying her neck and the make-up her maids had used to cover the marks of yesterday's encounter. "*Hmm*. It looks like you took my advice." He smiled at her, and she felt the urge to spit him in his eye.

"O-Of course, your Highness." She hated herself for stuttering. Why couldn't she stand up for herself, instead of sounding like a helpless puppy.

"Your Highness!" Chilian finally came over and placed himself between the prince and Aimee. Maxim stared at him for a minute, and then let go of Aimee's jaw. She hadn't realized that she had been on her toes until she fell back on her feet. Chilian quickly grabbed her arm and forced her in behind him.

"Your Highness, maybe you shouldn't handle a noble woman in such manners," he explained in a surprisingly calm voice, "your relationship with the Duke of Edenran is already in shambles. How do you think he would react if he had seen this?"

"Are you threatening me, cousin?" Maxim asked intrigued.

"Of course not. I would never. I just wouldn't want you to ruin your chances of a good friendship with the east any more than it already is." Aimee could feel Chilian's hand shake around her arm. He was playing with the devil, and he knew it.

Prince Maxim smiled coldly and played along. "You're right." He squinted his eyes, looked over Chilians shoulder and the cold dead smile turned sinister and bitter. "Lady Aimee?"

"Yes, your Highness?" Her voice was small, nothing but a whisper.

"Are you hungry?"

It felt like an invisible punch to the face.

He was mocking her, and he enjoyed it to the fullest. And now he mentioned it, she was starving, and it felt terrible the more she thought about it. She despised the prince's power over her.

She shook her head and stared at the ground. She didn't realize that she had been holding on to Chilian's back before now, but she didn't move her hand.

Maxim looked satisfied and reached into a pocket in his pants. He grabbed a round object wrapped in a small handkerchief. He unwrapped the bundle and in his hand he was holding a small bun. It looked newly baked and the smell of it quickly made Aimee's teeth run.

Chilian stared confused, from the bun to the prince, and back again. "What is this?" he asked, while tightening his grip around her arm. It was starting to hurt a little.

"A little present if you could say that. I had meant to drop it off, but you can just have it now. Here, Doll. Take it." He held his hand out in front of her and with shaking hands, she carefully took the warm bun. She wanted to just swallow it whole, but remembered how bad that would look. So, she just stared at it.

Maxim's smile turned sweet. Like he was looking at a loved one opening a present or like a Mother staring at her child. It freaked her out and made her even more uncomfortable.

"Leave us," he said and the smile turned to a completely unfaced expression.

"E-Excuse me...?" Aimee asked in confusion.

"No questions, Doll. Go now. You have packing to do, right?" His eyes pierced through her, and the icy cold of them almost froze her completely.

This time she wouldn't make the same mistake as the night before and bowed deeply. "Of course, your Highness."

She started walking away, but Chilian grabbed her shoulder. "Wait! What is going on? What's the bun about?"

"It's none of your business, cousin." The prince interrupted. "Now let go and let her scram. And don't go looking for her after."

Chilian wasn't looking at him. He stared at Aimee tormented, confused, and desperate all at once, begging her to stay and answer his questions.

She couldn't take him looking like that, so she stepped forward and wrapped her arms around him in a sincere hug. He was surprised at first but returned her gesture and held Aimee tightly. It was a comforting feeling. It had been so long since she had hugged anyone.

His arms were muscular and warm around her, and she wanted to stay like that.

"Come tell me goodbye tomorrow."

"Of course…" Chilian whispered back, and his grasp around her tightened.

"Now, little doll!" the prince said impatiently.

Aimee let go and started walking away quickly. When she looked back, Chilian was looking longingly after her, and it felt like a little part of her heart shattered.

*

She turned a corner and disappeared into the main hall.

Chilian felt something missing, and her warm embrace already felt like a hundred years ago.

"Oh, stop it, you look like a lost puppy dog," Maxim said from somewhere behind him.

Chilian collected himself and stood up straight. And then he felt the anger roaring up inside of him. He had been screaming on the inside while he was forced to watch Maxim handling Aimee the way he did. He had almost drawn his blade at the crown prince, which in itself, was reason enough to be considered a traitor and killed.

Maxim stepped up beside him and they stood in silence for a while.

"Why did you feel the need to do that to her, your Highness?" Chilian asked calmly pretending to have collected himself. In reality, he was nearly exploding in anger. No one should be allowed to hurt his blossom like that.

"Why not? It's not like she had anything against it," Maxim simply replied. Chilian was fuming.

"She was clearly scared, your Highness." The words were so tightly squeezed out between his teeth, that they almost sounded like gibberish.

The prince simply sighed.

And then he walked away.

Chapter 5

Summer Days in Edenran

"Chili!"

He turned around at the sound of his name being shouted from afar. Chilian barely had time to prepare, before she launched at him, knocking them both to the ground. He landed hard on his back and was completely knocked out when Aimee landed on top of him.

"What are you doing?" he asked while trying to regain some kind of consciousness.

"Look at what I found down by the pond!" she said excitedly.

In her hand she held a small earing, with a broken piece of amber attached to it. "Isn't it pretty?" Chilian pushed Aimee off of him and took a closer look at the piece.

It wasn't anything special. Just a broken earring, some noblewoman probably lost without even noticing.

"Blossom, it's just an earring," he said.

Aimee turned red and snatched the jewel back.

"Well, I think it's beautiful. And it's prettier than any earring I've ever had."

And then it hit Chilian that she was right. Her damn father didn't care enough about her to buy her that kind of stuff. She said she was lucky to even have normal clothing and food which no daughter of a rich Archduke should ever have to say. His fists closed and a small anger burned up in him.

"Well, what are you doing?" Aimee asked, now distracted by a rose she had found in the bush behind him.

"I was looking for you actually," he started.

"Why?"

"I don't know. I guess I missed your stupid face." He laughed. Aimee turned even redder and tried to hit him, but he was quick on his feet and avoided her attacks easily like he had learned from Colyn.

His smile widened as she started chasing him around until she got tired, and collapsed back into the flower bushes.

Chilian ran over to sit beside her, grabbed Aimee by the shoulders, and gently pulled her into his arms. She went completely quiet in his embrace, and they sat like that for a long time, enjoying each other's presence and the sun's warm shine gracing their skin.

He wished he could stay there forever.

"And why are you so upset?"

Laurence's voice was like a needle piercing into Chilian's ears. After everything that had happened that afternoon, he did not need Laurence snooping around in his personal life right now.

After his meeting with Aimee had been cut short by Maxim, he had gone straight down to the training grounds where he now stood and molested a poor training dummy with his sword, to let out all his anger.

He had forgotten that Laurence always trained at this time of day too, and he was not pleasantly surprised.

Laurence Dahlian was probably his best friend. They had started training together under Colyn when Chilian turned nine, and they had been somewhat inseparable ever since.

He was blessed with long black hair, and acorn eyes. His skin was to the darker side, and even if his physique was kind of lanky, he still stood tall and proud besideChilian. He mainly wore purple or brown clothes, and he was never seen far from some fortunate servant's bedroom door.

They had been knighted at the same time, and now they both worked half time as instructors for the palace guards. They had come a long way together.

But damn, he could be a pain in the ass.

"It's none of your business," Chilian simply answered and continued his well-practiced swings.

"Maybe not. But it's rare to see you so worked up, so I can't help but wonder who pissed you off so much, that you're imagining their face on a training dummy." Laurence gestured to the almost shredded human bag of hay in front of them, and Chilian finally stopped his practice.

He let out a loud sigh and sat down on a conveniently placed haybale that stood up against the wooden fence. Laurence was quick to follow his example and sat down next to him.

"You remember the masquerade yesterday?" Chilian asked after a long silence.

"Well, not really, because I found a very nice butler, and we accidentally stumbled into a broom closet together. But I can imagine it was boring." Chilian rolled his eyes at him, but a smile did escape onto his lips.

"At the ball I danced with someone I haven't seen in a long time. And today we spend some of the afternoon together in the gardens. But—" Chilian paused not knowing how to tell him.

Laurence looked intrigued and clearly wanted to learn more, but Chilian didn't know how to explain the situation.

They went quiet for a long time, just staring at the other

knights, doing laps around the running track.

"Well, tell me how you know the person?" Laurence slithered out. "You've never told me you had a long-lost lover."

"We aren't lovers!" Chilian shouted startled just a tad too loud. He felt his cheeks burn, and he wanted to punch Laurence for suggesting that kind of connection so bluntly.

He calmed down and sighed.

"Do you remember when the palace was besieged by the rebellion ten years ago?" Laurence nodded, recalling the frightening night they were both forced to flee from their home.

"I was sent away with my mother to live on Sir Erlan Achillea's estate in Leirath while the situation here got under control—" Chilian paused for a moment, remembering his mother barging into his room one night, with distress in her eyes. "While I was there I met the duke's youngest daughter. She had always been lonely, so she was thrilled to have someone there, roughly her own age... We would always play together out in the flower field behind their mansion, and Laurence, let me tell you I have never met anyone like her," he said with a sudden passion taking over his speech, "she was always so cheerful and funny, and when I was with her I felt like a normal boy. Not the son of an archduke. Not the king's nephew. I didn't feel alienated or resented for my status. We were just children, playing in a field. She was so kind, and she had all of these dreams about living normally. She knew a ton about plants and common life, outside of titles and mansions, and she was just a pure ball of joy running around."

Chilian laughed quietly, as he remembered all the good times they'd had together. It felt like that time was centuries away now... "I distinctly remember that she would always make a bouquet with flowers representing her family. And one day she came up to me and showed me how she had added a dark blue one, because of my eyes. She said she saw me as much as family as her father… She was everything to me back then. She still is. So, I made an oath, to protect her to the best of my abilities. But…"

Chilian paused.

Laurence stared at him, impatiently waiting for a continuation, but it was like a rope had been tied around his neck and made it a struggle to breathe. Laurence shifted his legs and started looking worried, so Chilian forced himself to go on.

"At the start of spring she got sick. Really sick… I don't know what it was, but she would be asleep for days at a time, and never have any energy, to even walk. I always sat in her room, watching over her, and in the morning I would pick flowers for her. Whenever she was awake, she was in pain, and I think everything seemed like a blur to her. She never knew where she was or who was with her." Chilian started tearing up, thinking about what she must've felt in those hours. He hated himself for having just sat on a chair next to her, instead of doing something about it. "The worst part though, was that no one from her family ever visited her. It was always just me, and her nanny. Once a day a physician would have a look at her, and sometimes my mother would check up on us too, but neither her father nor her sister cared."

Chilian felt the anger rising up inside of him again. He had a sudden urge to take his sword and swing it at the dummy's head again, pretending it to be Sir Erlan's face.

"I've never heard of her until now," Laurence said quietly. "She has never been to court before, has she?"

"No not officially, I don't think," Chilian responded, "she always wanted to get away from the nobility and the status she held. Just live a normal life. So I think she kept her distance on purpose."

Laurence simply sighed deep in thought.

"I had to return to the palace before she recovered," Chilian finally said, "they had to drag me out of her room. I fought them the entire trip back to the palace. I was never allowed to visit her again…"

The man sat in silence, reflecting on the story. The light touch of the wind gave Chilian goosebumps. The sounds of the sand blowing away beneath him, and people running around on the track, combined with the orange sunset made the entire scenery feel somber.

"Do you want to know the worst part?" Chilian asked.

Laurence hesitated. "I don't think I do but tell me anyway." He let out a nervous laugh and shifted his legs again.

"After a few months I got word that she had officially recovered. But apparently the medication she had been taking had induced some kind of amnesia. She struggled with extreme memory loss, or something like that. but I didn't think it was that bad… But she has no idea of our time together…"

A single tear managed to escape Chilian's eye. He wiped it away quickly and prayed Laurence hadn't noticed.

"So, she doesn't remember…"

"No."

"And yet you danced together?"

"I managed to ask her previously. She was lost in a hallway and asked for help." He laughed.

"Ah."

Silence.

It was weird just sitting together without a single word being exchanged. The sun was setting, and its orange light painted everything in a golden color. They usually never had peaceful moments like that together, so it was nice for a change.

Laurence shifted again.

"And why were you so angry just now?"

Chilian's grip around the sword's handle tightened at the question. The small emerald pommel at the tip, looked squeezed in his hand.

"I managed to ask her on a walk through the gardens, but my cousin cut it short… He harassed, *hurt* her, and called her *'his doll'.*" The sick nickname burned on his tongue, and if you looked close enough, you could see the smoke coming out of his ears. "There was also this weird moment when he asked if she was hungry and gave her a freshly baked bun. He sent her away and told me to leave her alone for the rest of the day."

Laurence wrinkled his nose in confusion. "He has always been an asshole," he declared.

"You could be executed for that comment."

"Famous last words."

They smiled.

"So, what are you gonna do about it?" Laurence suddenly asked in a somber voice.

"I don't know. She's leaving again tomorrow, so she should be safe from him afterwards."

"Are you going with her?"

Chilian felt a knife stabbing him in the chest, and twisting. She was leaving, maybe for good, and he had no way of seeing her. His own father, Archduke Renan, had forbidden him to leave the palace, since he was second-in-line to the throne, and the only heir to Stillgate. If he died on some stupid outing to see Aimee, the Malvaria family would lose all chances of taking the crown, and they would resent *her* for it.

And he knew that she probably wasn't coming back to the palace after the prince's harassment, so he wouldn't have a chance at encountering her like he did that time in the hall. He wouldn't be able to see nor protect her. She would be all alone in her miserable mansion with people that treated her like dirt. He couldn't stand the idea. He didn't want to lose her again. He had already failed her once.

"I have to go."

Chilian stood up and walked away. He had so many thoughts and all he wanted was to be alone and collect them all.

So he left Laurence behind and on the haybale and didn't bother to finish his training.

Chapter 6

A Flower in A Cage

She felt the warmth of the summer sun shining on her face through the window.

It reminded her of her nanny's gentle touch from when she was younger, and she didn't want to move away from it.

But she snapped back to reality when her stomach started rumbling again. She had officially gone two entire days without eating.

The bun Maxim had given her was untouched. Knowing him, Aimee didn't want to risk anything, so it just sat on the small coffee table teasing her endlessly.

She felt weak and her head was spinning. The maids had started packing all of her things and in a few minutes, she would be on her way. She had asked Lilly to pack some food from the kitchen, and as soon as they were out the gate she would dig in.

Her other maids Sheldy and Linari were running around her room, packing up everything, and efficiently putting every single piece of silk and cotton clothing neatly together in the bags.

Aimee took a sip of the sweet tea in her cup and looked out over the gardens again. She could see a couple of nobles walking around, enjoying the late afternoon hours. It was peaceful.

Her maids finally ended packing and Lilly returned from the kitchen with a basket of bread, cheese, and a little fruit.

The kitchen staff had only let her get away with it, because the chefs didn't recognize her as Aimee's maid. Linari said that if they had known, it would have been reported straight to the prince.

When everything was packed and ready Aimee and the maids started their tour to the courtyard where a carriage should be waiting for her.

She was wearing a warm-blue dress, with a broad neckline revealing her shoulders and small butterflies decorating the hem.

The skirt flowed nicely, and the trim was sewn with golden thread. It was definitely one of her better dresses.

It was standard and simple, quite fitting for her departure.

But when she walked out of the great doors, down to the courtyard she had admired a few days before when she arrived, it wasn't a carriage, but ten soldiers that met her.

In front of them stood the prince, smiling coldly at her. He was wearing a blue uniform, and a white cape, that swayed gently in the wind around him.

Aimee stopped dead in her tracks.

Had he discovered the food? Or was he offended by something she had done? Had her maids told him she hadn't eaten the bun?

"Your Highness. What do I owe the honor?" she asked carefully.

"Well, I'm a bit hurt, Doll. That you were just gonna leave me here, without saying goodbye..." he explained. The nickname sent a shiver down her spine, and it was like it choked her.

It didn't help that he suddenly started walking towards her with long, calm steps. She wanted to move backwards, away from him, but she stood strong and didn't move a muscle.

Prince Maxim stopped right in front of her and inspected Aimee's expression. "You truly look like a little doll," he mumbled. His hand reached out for her cheek and the touch sent an even bigger wave of shivers down her spine. She couldn't help but flinch at the feeling of his cold fingers on her skin and Maxim seemed to enjoy the sight of her in terror. "I've decided to keep you here."

Aimee's heart skipped a beat.

"What…?"

"I'm gonna keep you here like a little pet." He smiled warmly at her, but all she felt was disgust.

"What – You can't do that," she snapped at him, but Maxim reacted quickly and grabbed her by the back of her neck.

She heard her three maids gasping behind her, and the soldiers started moving uncomfortably, not sure of what to make of the situation.

"I can actually," he mumbled, "I own you now. You belong to me. You do as I tell you. Understood?"

Panic spread rapidly through her body, and she tried to get away from him, while keeping her sight straight and not burst into tears. She felt sick and really tried to get away from his grip but found herself uselessly crying instead.

"You never usually struggle like this? Is the thought of me that disturbing?" Prince Maxim asked in a sinister voice. She wanted to spit him in his ugly face.

"You'll be staying near my quarters from now on, so I've already prepared an apartment for you. You will in addition to this receive two more servants, and a seamstress will come later to take your measurement for a new wardrobe. You three—" She heard her girls stiffen as they realized that they now were involved, and Sheldy took the lead.

"Yes, your Highness?" she asked.

"Your Highness, this isn't what I want," Aimee mustered.

"Do you think I care?" Maxim looked her dead in the eyes. He was serious. She wanted to scream. How long would he hold her here? What would he do to her? Would she ever see her father again? Or her sister? And what about Chilian?

Maxim said something to Sheldy, but she didn't hear it.

So many thoughts were spinning around her head, that she didn't notice Maxim also giving an order to his soldiers. Suddenly, two large men came over and grabbed both her arms.

Fear struck in. She struggled to try and free herself, but the men's grasps only tightened and the more she struggled the more it hurt. She yelled and screamed at them to let her go, but the soldiers looked unfazed.

"Bring her along now," Maxim said, and the entire parade started moving. The prince led the way, followed by Aimee and the two men. Then the rest of the soldiers followed behind and lastly her maids that frantically tried to keep up, not understanding anything of what was happening.

It must have been a weird sight.

She saw multiple nobles looking concerned as they moved through the big corridor with the struggling Aimee screaming for help. At one point she even saw the princess, Sofeel, looking their way with a terrified look in her eyes. She was with the same woman as at the party.

Aimee eventually stopped struggling and was almost dragged by the two soldiers up the stairs. She kept slipping in her skirt, so she just let her legs follow behind her. They went past the second floor and continued to the third. That place was usually off limits, due to it being the royal family's private space, so she was naturally even more confused than earlier.

She suddenly heard someone running behind them.

"AIMEE!"

She recognized Chilian's voice immediately. She turned her head to look at what he was doing here and was surprised to see him running straight towards them.

The soldiers blocked his way to her, but he athletically knocked most of them over and moved past the rest with an almost unnatural speed.

He was almost there, but without a warning a loud thud was heard, and Chilian fell to the ground. One of the guards outposted near a door had hit him with the back of his sword, and now Chilian was roaming around on the floor trying to get back up after the impact.

"Chilian!" she yelled, wanting to run to him, but the soldier on her right quickly covered her mouth, enabling her speech movement.

He was right there in front of her, injured, and she couldn't reach him. She could feel the tears streaming down her face, and she damned herself for putting him in this situation. He didn't have to be a part of this. *Why would he bother for someone like her, of all people?*

A soldier came up behind him and got him back on his feet. He kept Chilian's arms behind his back, and another soldier came up and removed his sword, and a small knife hidden in his boot, to make sure he wasn't a danger to anyone.

"Well, well, well, if it isn't my cousin." Maxim smiled maliciously and walked in between them. "That was a pretty dumb attempt at a confrontation, wasn't it? Where are your manners?"

Chilian, who had somewhat regained consciousness stared at the prince with murder in his eyes.

"What are you doing to her?" he asked, with his teeth shut tight. He was angry.

"Why do you worry for such a thing? It's none of your business anyway."

"You can't just take a person as you wish! You can't treat her like this!"

Chilian was yelling now, and it sent a shiver down her back. He was actively raising his voice at the crown prince. Was he trying to be killed?

Aimee finally managed to get her mouth free of the soldier's hand for a brief moment.

"Chilian, It's okay! Don't worry about me!" she pleaded. "Don't get involved in this, I beg you."

Chilian looked disbelieving at her, and Maxim broke out into a sinister laughter. "Well would you look at that? The doll is actively sending her rescue away. She already knows who her master is."

Chilian's eyes were fuming. He struggled to get free of the men's grip but to no avail.

Maxim's smile faded and left only a bored demeanor. "Bring him to the main hall and keep him at the bottom of the stairs until I say otherwise."

"Yes, your Highness," an old soldier with a white beard said hesitantly.

The biggest of the soldiers took charge and the group split up into two. Aimee helplessly watched Chilian being taken down the stairs while fighting immensely as if he were on his way to the chopping board. His eyes met hers with a terrified expression one last time. And then he was gone.

Maxim sighed and continued walking down the hall. He stopped in front of a big blue door, beautifully decorated with golden birds and white snowflakes.

The maids opened the door, and the room that met her was

massive. It looked just like the room she had stayed in previously, but everything was just scaled up to a ten.

The walls were decorated with golden patterns and the furniture were of the utmost luxury. Everything was detailed and shiny, it almost hurt just looking at it.

Once again there was a big opening hall with a table in the middle leading out to a balcony. To the right was a big office, with so many books, you could almost call it a library on its own.

The master bedroom looked worthy of a queen, and she felt so small when compared to the giant canopy bed. Instead of Achillea, blue hydrangeas decorated the room's walls, and lent way to the name, The Blue Chambers.

Maxim stopped in front of a lounge area with blue couches, bookshelves, and a marble fireplace. All the edges and the surface were covered in gold, creating elaborate circular patterns down the sides and on the shelf above it.

"Let go of her and get out. I wanna talk privately with my toy."

The soldiers loosened their grasp of her arms, and she went tumbling to the ground, realizing how hard they had been holding onto her. She looked back over her shoulders and saw everyone leave the room, even her maids. Lilly quietly glanced back at her, and Aimee gave her a desperate look, but there was nothing she could do. The door closed behind her, and they were alone.

Aimee took a deep breath and tried to sound calm. "Your Highness. May I ask what you're achieving by bringing me here…?"

There was a short silence.

Then he started walking in a circle around her. Inspecting her. Like a hawk watching over its prey, waiting to strike. She could feel her body shaking. The constant sound of his black shoes against the cold stone, was the only sound to be heard in the large room.

"Answer me, please!" she shouted out of frustration. The footsteps stopped somewhere behind her, and she completely froze. She had nowhere to run, nowhere to hide. She knew no self-defense, and the man behind her was so unpredictable and ruthless, that a simple word could be the end of her.

"I'm sorry, I didn't mean to raise my... I just find this situation very biza—"

"Be quiet," he snapped.

She flinched at the hard voice, her hands shaking beyond belief.

Maxim let out a soft sigh and moved over to the couch. He sat down calmly on the soft cushions and crossed his legs.

"Sit over here, doll," he said and pointed to the floor in front of him. He wanted her to sit like a dog? Probably to humiliate her and feel good about himself.

She wanted to throw up. Everything she had learnt about pride and honor told her not to do it, but she couldn't risk her life over her stupid dignity.

Aimee stood up and walked over to Maxim, refusing to even look at him. Although she could feel his lazy smile burn directly through her.

She stopped in front of him, keeping her gaze at the floor.

"Sweet doll, I said sit." He leaned forward on the couch, clearly losing his patience. She didn't want to risk an early death, so she finally sat down. Maxim smiled with a pleased look in his eyes.

She was disgusted.

"Get me that platter over there, will you Dear?" he asked in a calm tone. She looked over at the small table behind her and saw a platter with lots of different foods on it. There were small cakes, a variety of fruits, biscuits and cookies, different kinds of sauces, breads, and buns.

She felt her teeth swimming in water and her stomach rumble at the sight. She hadn't eaten for so long and here was some of the most delicious snacks she had ever seen in a long while. A punch to the gut probably wouldn't hurt as much as it did having to look at it without indulging.

She took the platter and held it up for prince Maxim. Aimee expected him to take it from her, but instead he started eating from her hands. She felt so ashamed about the fact he had such power over her and hated him for doing this to her.

The worst thing though was that he was eating right in front of her. Teasing her with the smells and sights of the delicious desserts and bread. Her stomach was now loudly rumbling and the hunger she felt was overwhelming.

She must have looked ridiculous because the prince started giggling affectionately at her. He bent over her and gently touched her cheek while smiling.

"Are you hungry, doll?" he asked.

She couldn't help but nod at his remark, and a victorious expression folded around his face. He picked up a single grape and held it up to her mouth. She knew how embarrassing it would be to her family's name if anyone saw this, but she couldn't help herself. She took a bite of the grape, and the sweet flavor brought her to tears.

She chewed the fruit slowly, appreciating the taste to the fullest.

The prince smiled satisfied and continued feeding her. It was humiliating and awkward without either of them speaking, although the prince seemed to greatly enjoy their time together.

Before long the food slipped up, and they sat in silence for a while.

Eventually, Aimee had had enough of it and decided to break the silence. "Can I ask a question, your Highness?"

"Call me Maxim. That title has no place in your pretty mouth. Besides, it's fun to hear my name in a casual setting," he said, entertained.

How could he say that?

Calling a future monarch by their first name was usually only done by parents or partners. It wasn't just a thing people did. It was seen as a great offense by some.

"Is that really necessary...?"

"Do you want to eat again, or would you rather I teach you your place?"

He sounded cold, and his eyes hardened as he spit the words in her face. She had no choice.

"M-Maxim." The name burned in her throat, and she wanted to spit it out and never have to deal with it again. "Can I ask you...?"

The prince thought for a while but gave her permission.

"Do I just live here now? When will I be allowed home? Will I see my family again?"

"Those answers will come with time," he responded calmly.

"But why me? Why do I have to be kept in here and treated like a dog...? What have I done that I haven't yet repaid for?"

Maxim stared at her. She couldn't determine his expression. He looked thoughtful and confused, but also victorious. It was scary how good he was at masking his thoughts and emotions.

"I've never met anyone like you," he started, "at first you had no clue who I was. You had no idea of my status. You called me like any ordinary noble, and I guess that simply intrigued me.

You're beautiful, with exotic features and your eyes remind me of the forest. I've always loved the forest…" He once again stroked her cheek and the touch felt like burns ripping open her skin.

"And so, you're just gonna keep me here?"

"Of course. I couldn't let you go even if I wanted to. You're too valuable. You will prove quite useful in the future. And there's just something about you. The way you're denying me, when every other woman I've known, quite literally throws themselves at me. No manners. No prohibitions. It's disgusting. You're not like that."

"But I want to go home…" she cried, frustrated by his selfishness.

"This is your home from now on, doll. You belong to me. And you'll do as I say, or you'll go without food. You'll say what I want. Wear what I want. And eat what I want. If at all that is."

"You're sick," she said with spite, and the smile on his face turned twisted and sinister, almost inhumane.

"Maybe I am. But that definitely doesn't help your situation." He grabbed her chin for the third time, and gently placed a kiss on her forehead.

"Your maids will bring you some comfortable clothes to wear and guards will be posted outside your door, so don't even think of leaving. That seamstress should also be here at any minute now. Do as I tell you and your stay will be very pleasant, I assure you."

He stood and walked over to the door. And just as suddenly as he had taken her prisoner, he disappeared out into the palace halls.

Leaving her on the floor alone, and without any idea of how much her life had been turned on its head in a single afternoon.

Chapter 7

An Empty Platter of Grapes

Maxim came strolling down the stairs without a worry on his face. He looked pleased, and the sight of his smug smile, made the flame in Chilian's stomach rise to an inferno. He had been alone with Aimee for almost an hour, and the fear of whatever he had done to her scared him beyond belief.

He felt the urge for murder as the prince slowly descended down the stairs with his signature pearly whites visible to the entire world. He couldn't hold back his anger any longer. "Maxim, you son of a bitch!" he yelled at the top of his lungs. Everything went quiet. Maxim even stopped halfway through his descent to the main floor, and the shocked expression on his face was surprisingly satisfying. "What did you do to her you sick bastard…?" Chilian whispered through his teeth in pure rage.

The prince's shock turned into an arrogant grin before him, and Maxim simply continued walking. He stopped in front of Chilian and smiled the way only he could.

Maxim leaned in over Chilian and quietly whispered in his ear.

"I think she enjoyed it…"

Everything came crashing down.

Chilian could feel the blood draining from his face and his legs failing under his weight.

"Don't try to come near her. For your own sake," he said.

Maxim let out a single laugh and then he was off. The soldiers finally let go of him and Chilian tumbled to the ground.

He had failed her. Again. That swine had done unforgiving things to her and where was he?

His despair once again turned into anger faster than he thought possible. The adrenaline kicked in and he was off. He ran as fast as he could, through courtyards, over garden paths, down to the training grounds.

He knew that the only quarters available closest to the prince's, was a guest room called The Blue Chambers, specially intended for lovers of the crown prince to stay over in. Either that or Maxims own quarters. Chilian also knew that Maxim probably had placed guards, both on the stairs to the third floor, and in front of the doors. So there were only one other possible way in.

He ran out of a side door with a silver handle the soldiers used for guard shifts and past the horse stables on the right. He stumbled into the equipment shed on the training grounds and crashed open the secret door, hidden behind a wall of wooden shields.

Laurence jumped three meters in the air at the loud crash, and the girl under him turned white at the fact they had been discovered.

"Chilian, what the hell—"

"Laurence, I don't have time for whatever you're doing, I need your help!"

"What—"

But before Laurence could properly respond or even put his shirt back on, Chilian was already gone on his way to the Servants Corridor. He could hear Laurence yelling at him, but he had no time to explain. He had already wasted enough time just standing around.

They reached a giant hallway in the basements where usually only servants were allowed. The long corridor was aligned with small doors, leading to various staircases. Each staircase led to different rooms in the palace, allowing easy access for maids and other servants. This was the only way. The door he was looking for was at the very end of the hall.

After a while of sneaking around, trying to not be spotted by the servants doing their tasks, he finally reached the end and read the signs above. *Kings Apartments, Queens Apartments, Princess's Quarters, Prince's Quarters.* And finally, *The Blue Chambers.* He opened the door and looked over his shoulder to see Laurence looking confused, frightened and a bit out of breath, all at the same time. Chilian had never acted like this before, so it was understandable.

"I need you to keep a lookout from the inside of the door. If anyone tries to get in, keep it shut and make them believe it's locked. Don't let anyone in." Then without warning he turned around and started ascending the stairs.

"Wait, Chilian!" Laurence aggressively whispered behind him, but he didn't have time to explain. He rushed all the way up the narrow staircase, to the third floor and finally reached the door, all the while hearing Laurence's confused whispers from far below him.

Finally, he reached the tiny door leading to the room he believed to be Aimee's quarters.

But against his expectation, he hesitated at the door. He had imagined himself barging through it, and entering the room heroically, but he was scared. He was scared of what awaited him on the other side. Was she crying on the floor? Would she run to him and crumble in his arms? Or... Was she hurt? What if she was laying cold on the floor and...

No. He refused to finish the thought.

He reached for the door's rusted silver handle and turned it slowly.

What met him on the other side was definitely unexpected.

The room was painted orange in the setting sun's light and Aimee was sitting quietly on the floor in front of a blue couch. In her hand she was holding a silver platter with the remnants of grapes and bread. She was still fully dressed, and her hair wasn't in any way ruffled, so maybe his worst fear wasn't the case after all.

"Aimee…?"

The sound of his voice made her jump in surprise, and she turned around to find the source of his voice. Her eyes widened at the sight of him coming out through the hidden door in the wall. And as he got closer a painful expression appeared on her face.

Chilian could feel the tears pressing on his eyes and he had to do his hardest not to storm over, wrap his arms around her and hold her close. Instead he sat down next to her on the floor.

"What happened…?" he asked, terrified of what response she would give him. But instead of answering she sat quiet for a while. Just staring at him in disbelief.

"How did you get past the guards…?" she asked in a weak voice.

"I used the servant's secret stairs."

"Oh…"

She looked defeated. Broken. Like all happiness had been sucked from her world. A complete mirror to the happy and witty girl he had spent yesterday with.

And then the tears finally started falling.

"Aimee, I am so sorry. I shouldn't have let them take you

away, I should've protected you instead of letting that bastard do something like this to you, I should have fought harder, I'm—"

He didn't get to finish before Aimee jumped at him, wrapping her arms around his neck. She started crying into his shoulder, tightening her grip around him. He couldn't help but join her in the absolute despair she had faced all alone. She was warm as he held her close in arms.

A long while passed by.

She slowly slid down between his legs, and leaned up against his chest. She seemed comforted by letting him hold her like a child seeking an escape from the world.

His grip around her only tightened as the thoughts of whatever she had gone through appeared and disappeared in his mind. He wanted to hold her like that forever. To protect her from whatever dangers she would face and to fend off whoever came close to her. She was still that fragile little girl he had known all those years ago. It was like he was back in the chair by her bed, only able to watch as she dealt with her pain. He still loved her too much to see her suffer like that.

He wanted her for himself. Wanted to see her smile at the sight of him and wanted to destroy everything that threatened that ideal scenario.

But what he wanted most in that moment was to make Maxim suffer under his boot.

The sound of his screams slowly being suffocated under the weight of it.

But revenge would have to wait.

After a while the sound of the cries slowly vanished, and they were left to silence.

He was sitting with his back to the side of the couch and

Aimee was resting her head on his chest. He could feel her breath slowing down.

She moved her legs and gently started stroking his arm that was holding her close. "Are you ready to talk about it…?" he whispered.

Aimee was quiet for a long time, and he feared he had made a mistake in asking. But she opened her mouth and spoke in a small voice.

"He said he wants me as a sort of pet…" Chilian felt his muscles stiffening by the sentence. "He told me to sit on the floor in front of him and explained some of his reasoning, which were questionable in itself," she said in a disgusted tone, "and then, he started hand feeding me like a damn dog…" She pulled her knees up to her chest and rested her chin on them trying to look as small as possible.

Chilian was once again fuming. He almost couldn't speak through his tightly shut teeth. "Did he touch you…?"

Aimee moved uncomfortably in his arms. "He kissed my forehead," she said bluntly.

"I'm gonna murder him."

"Wait, no—"

"Too late. He's done for." Chilian buried his head in her hair, trying to hold back the urge of storming out the door, and throwing Maxim out of a window on the third floor.

A faint chuckle escaped her lips and the happiness he felt over the fact that she could still joke in such a bizarre situation was overwhelming. Almost overshadowing his previous more murderous thoughts.

He sighed.

"Seriously though. I'll get you out of this. I won't let him hurt you…"

"You can't promise that."

"I can, actually. I won't let him."

"And how would you stop him from doing anything?"

He went quiet.

"Why do you even care?" she asked, "you've only just met me and yet you're ready to start a war with one of the most powerful men in Oplia. You'll get yourself killed over a stranger."

Silence.

He had to tell her. If not all of it, then just a little.

"I don't know if this is the greatest time to say this... But you are more important to me than my entire family and all my titles combined..." he whispered hesitantly. He didn't want to reveal everything all at once. He feared she might already be too confused and scared to understand it. He wanted to tell her when the time seemed right, and now wasn't it.

"You keep talking about me like we've met before. Is that the case?"

She looked up at him with those beautifully curious, turquoise eyes, and his heart skipped a beat.

"In a way. I met you a long time ago... Although I don't believe you remember," he whispered, "I do though... But I'd rather tell you later when all of this with Maxim has settled down." Her big eyes widened and were too interested to ignore. He gently placed a hand over them, blocking her view and giving him a chance to think clearly. Chilian felt his face return to a somewhat normal temperature and continued, "I don't want you to worry, okay? This isn't the time to dump it all on you. Just know that I would do more for you, than one would think."

"When was this?" she asked.

"Another time. I promise, Blossom." Her eyes widened at

the nickname. Like she had heard it before and saw small glimpses of their time together in her mind.

The expression was followed by a long silence. It seemed to indicate that she had understood the fact that he would tell her at a later point, although he could see she wasn't happy about it.

She slowly grabbed his hand. Gently she led it up to her lips and Aimee planted a soft kiss on the back of it.

Chilian felt a rush through his body and his face was once again burning.

"Thank you for coming all this way to see me. But you'll have to go now; the maids will be coming soon…" she said, unfazed.

He was taken aback by the sudden remark.

He didn't want to go. He didn't want to leave her in such a desperate situation. He felt his arms tightening around her and his expression turned serious.

He had to think of something. A plan to get her out. Chilian looked around the room and tried to use his brain that had been trained for this kind of quick planning. Anything to help her. And then the idea struck.

"Tonight. When everyone's sleeping," he said, "I'll go through the maid's staircase and bring you out of the palace. I'll get you some clothes and food and then take you as far away from this godforsaken place as possible. You'll get to live in a small village, without any pressure from the nobility, just like you've always wanted." It wasn't perfect, but it was the best he could do at the time.

Aimee looked at him confused.

"How do you know that I want to live as a commoner…?" she asked.

"You told me once."

"Really? And you would do that for me...?" she said skeptical.

He nodded.

Aimee went quiet for a very long time. Possibly thinking about the possibility of a quick escape to a better life.

"No..." she whispered.

"No?"

"I can't ask this of you. I won't let you risk your life for me," she said in a determined voice.

"Aimee what are you talking about? You can't stay here, you'll die," Chilian said, confused and scared about her sudden decision.

"Listen to me," she whispered.

She had turned around and now stood on her knees in between his legs to get higher up and give her a sense of authority. The warm blue dress with the small butterflies ruffled as she moved, and the big amount of fabric made it look like she was sitting on a blue cloud. She firmly laid her hands on the side of his neck and held his head in a comforting embrace. But her face looked firm. Tired and angry and scared. All at once. But it was the determination that shined through it all, and silenced Chilian.

So he listened.

"If we leave and we're found, we'll both be executed," Aimee continued, "If we aren't discovered they'll blame our families and friends, and they'll take the punishment out on them. I can't let that happen. I care too much about the people around me, and you, most importantly. To see you all be tortured and killed for the sake of someone like me... I wouldn't be able to live with myself if I let such a thing happen. It's better to let one suffer, than ten innocent."

Tears started running down her face as she talked and Chilian too started feeling his vision getting blurry, as the salty water filled his eyes. *How did that little girl grow up to be such a brave woman?*

He gently covered Aimee's hands on his neck with his own, and even though it felt like a million needles piercing every part of his body at once, telling him to convince her otherwise, he couldn't help but admire the bravery in her eyes.

"Please let me help you… Let me save you…" he whispered, his voice trembling. But Aimee shook her head.

"We both have too much to lose… I don't need your saving. For once in my life I have to take care of my own mess."

"But he'll kill you…" Chilian said desperately.

Aimee's face made a painful expression. She knew that her life would be a living hell, but she held onto her decision.

Then she leaned in and wrapped her arms around his neck.

He could feel her body shaking against his, her breath following an unnerving pattern and he could do nothing but return the embrace.

For a while there was silence. It was only broken by the occasional sound of an escaped sub and fabric, rubbing against itself.

"You need to get out of here before the maids find you," she suddenly said and started moving away from him. But a panic struck Chilian. He grabbed her waist, and the surprise in her eyes was big. A slight blush covered her teary face, and he couldn't help but love the sight of her.

"I don't want to leave you…" he whispered again, even more desperate to keep her there in his arms. To think she had such power over his emotions was frightening.

She returned the gesture with a faint, painful smile. "Don't make it harder than it already is," she mumbled.

She leaned in over him, and like on his hand gently placed a kiss on Chilian's forehead.

As she took a last look at him, her eyes spotted the white surface of the pearl, sitting on his vest's neckline. A soft smile planted itself on her lips and her gentle eyes met his.

He was too focused on her gaze that he forgot to hold on to her, as she stood up and looked down upon him. How she could smile in a time like this, was beyond his knowledge, and he truly admired her strength.

She walked toward the door in the wall, and he clumsily stood up to follow her over.

A moment passed by, of him admiring her in the faint light of the moon that was slowly rising now.

"I'll return tomorrow," he said, "I'll do everything in my power to get you out of here. I won't save you... But I'll do anything you ask of me. I promise."

Aimee simply smiled. "Just be careful..." she whispered.

A last look between them. And Chilian was gone, down the stairs. He heard the door shut behind him, and on the way down he felt the sorrow turn to anger.

Laurence was still there and his confused look only added to the fire inside of him.

The small pearl hairpin burned against his chest, as a reminder.

Maxim would pay for this.

And he would personally make sure of it.

"Blossom...?"

He had heard the duke's screaming all the way from the library. Later he had seen Aimee storming by in the hallway outside. He had dropped everything and sprinted after her out the door to the garden.

He had lost sight of her after she had run in between the trees and had hidden in the fading orange leaves.

Chilian already knew where she was, so he wasted no time in getting to her. And he had been right. She was sat on the mossy bench, curled up into a sulking ball, by their pond.

They had stumbled upon it together a few weeks after he had arrived and had since used it as their secret hideout. They often held picnics and small tea parties there. He once accidentally smashed an expensive cup, and Aimee had laughed her heart out over it, and smashed her own, leaving small porcelain shards everywhere. Let's just say it wasn't completely safe sitting around on the ground.

But now she sat in her light blue dress, sulking. And he had no idea of how to comfort her.

The sight took his breath away, as if he had been hit in the stomach again by Colyn, and all air had left, leaving nothing but a pair of empty lungs, and a crumbling heart.

He was so used to seeing her cheerful and easy going, smiling every minute of the day. He couldn't bear it.

"Leave me alone," she cried in a shaky voice, but Chilian silently agreed with himself that leaving her alone like that wouldn't be the greatest idea...

So, he walked over and sat down beside her. Not saying anything, not doing anything, just being there, by her side.

And eventually the crying quieted down, and she leaned her head onto his shoulder for comfort. They were looking out over the pond, which more or less looked like a swamp. Definitely not the prettiest place ever, but still somewhere they could be alone.

"Are you ready to tell me why you stormed out the door?"

he asked.

Aimee was quiet for a long while, but eventually she gave in.

"Father is mad at me again..." Chilian felt his fists tightening by the mere mentioning of him. *"I just tried to hug him, and he pushed me, so I fell... He started yelling again and I just wanted to get away." A faint sniff came from her as she went over the scene again.*

Chilian hated the sound.

"He shouldn't have done that. You were just trying to be nice," he told her, but Aimee shook it off.

"I know he doesn't like my hugs, so I should have just left while he was still somewhat normal. It was my fault."

"A Father should love his daughter, period. No one should feel it's their fault their parents don't like hugs," he said with a mouth full of spite.

She didn't respond.

"Can I ask you a question...?" he said while trying to hide his anger. He could feel her faintly nod against his shoulder, so he continued.

"Why is he always so angry with you? And why is Elniba so mean all of the time?"

Silence.

"I'm sorry, I shouldn't have asked..."

"No, no, it's okay," she said, pausing for a moment. She was trying to find the right words in her mind, and it was obviously a difficult subject for her. So he gave her the time she needed and waited for her for a long time.

"...He says I killed Mother..."

"What?"

She chuckled at his shocked impression and kept going. "Apparently, she died while giving birth to me. And I guess,

Father never forgave me. Neither did Elniba. And it doesn't exactly help that I'm apparently the spitting image of her. Or that's Father says at least..."

"I've never liked either of them," he mumbled in anger. He could feel Aimee's laughter and couldn't help but smile at the small victory the sound was to him.

The laughter died out shortly after though, and the silence was only broken by a young duckling entering the water of the pond.

"Don't hate them, Chili. They're the only ones I got. And I love them," *she said in a saddened voice. Chilian thought about it for a moment and decided that it wasn't good enough for her.*

"Blossom."

"Yes?"

He gently took her hand and squeezed, before turning to look at her.

"From now on. You got me too..."

Chapter 8

A Brother's Pet

Chilian had left about an hour ago.

She already missed his warm and comforting embrace, as the five maids and a strict seamstress were swarming around her like flies around a rotting apple. She was standing on a small pedestal while they were taking measurements, planning out future hairstyles, and debating which colors would fit her best, things like that.

She was happy. Linari, Sheldy and Lily had all been able to follow this weird shift and were now helping the others around her.

They had all arrived shortly after Chilian had left through the small door in the wall and had now been at it, for about forty minutes. More than anything, she just wanted to lay down and sleep, for as long as possible. She was slowly trying to digest everything that had happened on that day and the things she now understood only led to more questions.

She was supposed to go home to her father, but was now instead the crown prince's private prisoner. Was she just gonna live here from now on? Would she ever return home? And what exactly would happen to Prince Maxim's relationship with Edenran when her father found out about this? Would her father even care? Probably not, she figured. He had never cared. It was more likely he saw this as a way of gaining power. Maybe he would finally view her as useful, for once. The thought made her sick to the stomach.

There was a lot to think about, and the maids talking so loudly all around her definitely wasn't helping. She was developing a headache, and she just wanted to hide under the covers in her own bed, back home.

But suddenly everything went quiet when a knock was heard from the door. Fear struck in as one of the new maids made her way to open it.

What if it was Maxim, coming to harass her again? Or a guard relaying some new stupid order. Something along the lines of, 'she's not allowed to drink anything for a day'. Or maybe Chilian's visit had been discovered? And someone was going to punish them?

Her blood ran cold by all the different reasons someone would be visiting her at this hour. Her head felt heavy, and her legs too weak to support the rest of her body.

But as the maid opened the door, Aimee was surprised to hear a woman's voice on the other side. "Leave us, please," the voice mumbled quietly. It was very gentle.

The maid quickly did a curtsy and told the rest of the servants to leave the room. She was now standing alone in the big room, in a long nightgown they had prepared for her. An expensive blue one with silver threads lining all the small details around the neck and sleeves.

She looked nowhere near presentable, and the nervous sweat forming on her neck didn't help calming her nerves.

The last maid finally left and the individual at the door stepped into the room with grace written all over her.

To her big surprise it was neither Maxim nor a female guard, but Princess Sofeel. Prince Maxim's older sister, and if not for her gender the rightful heir to the throne of Oplia.

Aimee had seen her from afar at the ball and just before in the hallway as she was being taken away, but up close she was even more beautiful than she would have imagined. With a tall, and steady figure, the long white-blonde hair hanging down over her shoulders as curtains, contrasting the very familiar Istatis eyes that both Chilian, and Maxim possessed, she looked almost fake. Like a marble statue, come to life.

She was indulged in a beautiful dark blue silk gown, covered in what looked like silver stars. *Just like the night sky*, Aimee thought to herself.

The sleeves were poofy and yet light-looking. The bodice was perfectly cut with a low hanging neckline, and multiple layers of ruffles running down the front.

She was the embodiment of elegance, beauty, and confidence. Maybe that was only natural for a person whose birth-right had been taken away just because of their gender, and by the never-ending battle for perfection against her brother.

Stories of their rivalry had spread all over the country, and she was told to be as coldhearted as Maxim, because of it.

And cold she looked as she slowly moved towards Aimee. She showed no emotion, and no indication of what she was there for. The perfect poker face if Aimee had ever seen one.

But what she didn't expect, however, was the sudden stop the princess made a few meters from her, slowly looking her up and down, without a single thought showing through her neutral expression.

Aimee quickly curtsied before the princess, not wanting to upset her. The only thing she could think of was the uncanny resemblance to Maxim. And Aimee knew that if she was anything like her brother, she would not want to upset her.

"Your Highness. What do I owe the honor of your company...?"

Without daring to look up before permission, she listened to the slow, calm breath coming from Sofeel. But instead of a cold command or smug remark, a gentle hand was lightly placed on her shoulder.

"So you're the poor soul my brother has taken for himself..."

A warmth swept through Aimee's body as the words left the princess's mouth. In a glimpse she looked up to see a remorseful face looking at her with sadness in her blue Istatis eyes.

"I-I was lucky to be chosen by the prince," she said, not wanting to upset her, in case the painful expression was nothing but a mask covering her true intentions.

"Don't lie to me. I've known him all of his life and never has he done anything remotely like this. I saw the way he took you by force at the front gates. And I saw how you fought back. There's nothing to hide. I am just here to apologize..."

Aimee stared at her with both disbelief and wariness, not sure of how this situation would evolve.

"Your Highness, you have nothing to apologize for..."

"Well, of course I do." said Sofeel with a stern voice. Aimee was taken aback by this sudden reaction from someone who had just a few moments earlier been the embodiment of court courtesy and class. "I've never liked my brother," she continued, "but I shouldn't have just stood by and watched an innocent woman get taken for some sick pet against her will. I should have intervened and gotten you a chance to escape, or at least hide. Now, there's nothing I can do, and you'll be held here till Maxim either gets tired of you or—" The pause made Aimee shiver. "I don't think either of which will happen anytime soon, sadly..."

Aimee was stunned. Sofeel was right. The only way she was leaving this place was most likely in a casket. She would never return home to her pond in the garden. She felt herself tear up by the thought.

"Has he hurt you in any kind of way? Touched you perhaps…?" Sofeel asked.

"No, nothing serious."

Sofeel looked intensely at her. "Are you sure?"

"Yes, your Highness."

"Don't call me that." she said in a disturbed voice.

"But—"

"No." Sofeel's sorrow eyes had become serious and Aimee felt a chill crawl down her spine. She continued, "From now on I want you to be my equal. You're my sister from now on. And I don't want my sister talking to me like that," she said and grabbed Aimee's hand to hold it tightly. "Sofeel. From now on call me that, and nothing else. Even in public."

Aimee's eyes widened, as the words settled in her mind.

A sister.

She already had one of those. Elniba. But she had never considered her proper family. Elniba had always despised her, for taking away their mother. Always putting her down and blaming things on her. They had never played together nor spent more time than necessary in each other's presence. She and their father had always eaten separately not wanting to be reminded of what Aimee took from them.

The last time they had spoken was in the garden at home, when Aimee had passed her by on her way to the pond. A day before her departure to the palace. She had criticized Aimee's dress on the go and that had been all. Not a farewell, nor a letter.

It was sad that their last exchange had been an insult.

Elniba was probably about to arrive at her fiancé's mansion right about now, having traveled all the way from Edenran to Oldea on the other side of the country. An arranged marriage with the Archduke, Maulus Aquil. The two sisters would probably never see each other again...

The Oldea Duchy was so removed from both the other duchies and the country's politics that it was rare for them to appear at public events and no less host them.

It was only ever the Grand Duke Shanlor and his family that came as representatives for the other nobles in the area.

So a reunion between Aimee and her sister was not likely to ever happen.

But here was Sofeel, the princess of Oplia, sister to the crown prince, daughter of two powerful families standing before her, saying Aimee was her equal. Her sister. A thing no one had ever regarded her.

It was too much for her to handle, and she faintly felt her legs give in under her.

She didn't fall though, because before she could even think, Sofeel had wrapped her arms around her in an embrace. After hesitating Aimee returned the gesture and felt a single tear running down her cheek.

"Well, isn't this a lovely sight?"

The air was sucked out of Aimee's body by Maxim's cold voice.

It felt like Sofeel had the exact same reactions and quickly turned to bow before her brother.

He stood, leaned up against the doorframe, dressed in a very lazy suit, consisting of a half-buttoned shirt and a pair of loose pants. He looked fairly normal, for a change and the always tightly laid-back hair was now messy and seemed almost wet with all the hair gel he must've used this morning.

But no matter how normal his clothes looked, the sinister grin spread over his lips, was still the same as ever.

"Brother. I was welcoming your guest just now," Sofeel said in a surprisingly unfazed manner. Aimee couldn't begin to imagine the paranoia she must have faced, growing up with that madman.

"Sofeel, would you please leave us?"

She hesitated for a moment. When she started moving, panic struck Aimee and she reached out to grab Sofeel's hand, not wanting to be alone with that monster. But she could do nothing but give Aimee a sad glance and leave the room.

And she was once again alone with Maxim Istatis.

There was a long stretch of awkward silence between them before Maxim started walking over to her.

Without even realizing Aimee moved backwards, trying to avoid him when he reached out for her jaw.

"Don't be scared, doll," he said in a scarily gentle voice, "I know I've been extreme in the past, but it was only to show you who was in charge."

"Could it be possible to have a little alone time, perhaps...?" she asked, maybe a little too boldly. "Today has been... long."

The room fell silent.

"And why would my doll want to avoid my company?" He placed a relaxed hand on her chin, like embracing a loved one. But instead of the sweet feeling one would normally get, the touch felt like flames against Aimee's skin.

"It's just been a very long day, and I feel some alone time would help me process everything that's happened, your Highness..."

Instead of thinking about it, he looked at her with an

displeased expression. Aimee replayed her answer in her head looking for the mistake she so obviously had made, and she soon realized it. "I mean- M-Maxim…"

She felt acid filling her mouth by the word, but the prince once again looked pleased.

His gaze was cloudy, and Aimee couldn't figure out what he was thinking about. "Would it be possible to be alone though?" she asked again.

She heard the slam first. Then she felt her face burning. And then pain sat in.

She gently touched the side of her face Maxim had slapped. It was like the more time that went by, the clearer the situation became.

Then without warning, he grabbed her shoulders and violently pushed her up against the wall, behind them. She struggled, trying to escape his grasp, but it only seemed to hurt the more she moved.

Her head hit against the wall, and she felt the world faintly slipping for a moment before returning to reality.

"You don't get to request my presence and you do not get to request my absence," he said in a terrifyingly furious tone. This was the first time she had heard him like this. Angry. Fuming even. "I am the one in charge, and you'll do exactly as I tell you, no mistakes, no slip ups. I don't want you thinking this is a hotel where you can stay without meeting any demands! You belong to me, so you do as I please, understood?"

Aimee hesitantly nodded, tears streaming down her face, near inches away from his. She was scared beyond belief, longing for Chilian to break through the door in the wall, and take her from this awful place. Away from this awful man. She just wanted to escape. Down to her pond in the corner of her father's garden, hidden away from this cruel world.

"Do you understand?" he yelled in her face, snapping her back, from her comforting daydream.

"Y-yes!" Her voice was trembling, and she felt her entire body shaking.

The satisfied and calm expression returned to his face in an instant. "Good, doll. Don't cry though…" Again without warning, Maxim leaned in over her. He gently kissed her tears away, leaving nothing but a faint trail down her cheek.

Then he simply leaned his forehead against hers, and there they stood in complete silence, foreheads against each other. No words, no interaction. Just silence.

Aimee hated every second of his presence, but she wouldn't move in fear of him getting angry again. It was plain out humiliating. She wondered for a long time how her father would react to this. He always wanted her to be the ideal picture of an unfazed, pretty, noblewoman, and this was nothing like it.

A mess in a nightgown, tired, and with tears still silently rolling down her cheek, scared beyond belief, with a man using her as a headrest. She was a disgrace to the Achillea name, and she just wanted to end it all right then and there.

It was impossible to say how long they were standing.

It felt like hours, slowly slipping by. Before she knew it, the moon's calm light disappeared behind the clouds outside and they were left in the darkness of her room.

She couldn't imagine Maxim being comfortable standing there with his neck bent over her and his hands still steadily planted on her shoulders, against the wall.

But he didn't move an inch, and neither did she.

Chapter 9

Cracking Plans Like Eggs

"Laurence!"

He turned around by the shout of the name, and clearly wasn't prepared for the blade cutting through the air toward his face.

However, with a well-trained reflex, Laurence quickly raised his own sword to defend himself against Chilian's anger. His expression was filled with both terror and immediate concentration.

The rookies Laurence was instructing gasped in excitement, and suddenly a crowd had gathered around them.

"Whoa there, what has gotten into you?" he asked nervously, clearly surprised by his friend's sudden attack, but Chilian couldn't respond. The only thing he could think about was the anger and fear that was burning through his body, and the pain in his hands from the way he was clenching his sword.

He swung again and Laurence skillfully avoided. Again and again. But Chilian had always been superior in swordsmanship, so slowly he forced Laurence backwards. Swing after swing, his hits got more unhinged and deadly, and Laurence now clearly struggled to keep up with Chilian's blade.

He hit from above, the side, moved his legs accordingly, kept his stand straight, and delivered again and again.

Until a distinguished clang was heard.

A shock went through the crowd of onlookers as Laurence's blade split in two upon Chilian's strike.

He only barely managed to get out of the way of Chilian's sword with a maneuvered roll to the right.

Silence.

Chilian slowly lifted his head to see the crowd staring at him with unnerving faces. Most of them were clearly afraid and others had reached for their own swords. They all looked familiar, and he realized it was the team, him and Laurence had been training for a while. He cursed himself for having displayed such wrath in front of them and swore to do better in the future. This wasn't a way for a knight to behave.

"Twenty laps!" he simply yelled at the rookies, as he had done so many times before. And before he could collect his thoughts they were gone, only leaving behind a cloud of dust.

He stared for a while into the gravel he stood on before feeling, first a punch to the cheek and then pain filling his entire left face.

Chilian forced himself to minimize the expression of immense agony he felt and took it as calmly as he could.

"What the hell is wrong with you?" Laurence yelled in his face.

He was dirty after having rolled in the gravel and was now looking at him with murder in his eyes.

"I'm sorry…" he replied.

"You're sorry?" Laurence yelled, "you broke my sword! What has gotten into you?"

Chilian realized that it was the blade Laurence had gotten from his dad a few weeks before he passed from some kind of illness. They had never been close, but he still treasured it a lot, for its value and quality.

The guilt sat in quick after that.

Chilian was quiet. He wasn't even looking at Laurence. The only thing he had seen as he attacked his friend was that bastard's face.

"CHILIAN! *TALK TO ME!*" Laurence screamed, snapping him back to reality.

"I'm sorry!" he yelled back, looking straight into his dark, brown eyes. Laurence was pissed and with good reason.

Chilian felt the shame rushing in over him like a wave. He had humiliated him in front of their team, broken his father's sword and hadn't given a single warning before striking.

The anger, guilt, shame, and fear all mixed together in his head, and he turned around to walk away, and get himself under control. But before he had the chance he was stopped by a harsh hand grabbing his shoulder, and turning him around.

"You're not going anywhere, before you tell me what the hell is going on! Sit down!" Laurence yelled while pointing to the haybale where they, just a night before, had found a new kind of understanding for each other.

He tried shaking Laurence off, but he was having none of it. Before Chilian had realized, Laurence was dragging his ass along the sand and promptly sat him down, in their haystack.

He turned to stand in front of him and there they were.

Chilian was looking away afraid of the murderous stare Laurence was giving him and felt his own face burning up of embarrassment.

There was silence for a while, until Laurence decided it was enough.

"What did Maxim do this time?" he asked harshly.

Chilian didn't reply.

"Oh stop acting like a child and talk to me!"

Silence.

Laurence sighed. "It's about her, isn't it?"

Defeated, Chilian nodded.

After their meeting in The Blue Chamber, Chilian had told Laurence about it on their way back. Throughout the night anger had built more and more inside of him, before he could only see red. He just needed something to hit and let all the anger out on.

Laurence sat down beside him. The atmosphere was so thick you could cut it with a knife.

"I know you're mad about not being able to help her and all, but this is out of your control, okay? The best you can do is be there for her."

"What if the person in there was your sister, huh? You wouldn't just sit still like this and take it, would you?"

"I would be angry, yes. And with every fiber in my body wish death upon whoever did it. But I would hold it inside and keep both of us safe instead of running a rampage and scaring off all the rookies!" he said with anger.

Chilian was lost. He knew Laurence was right, and he didn't want to put Aimee in any more danger than she already was. But still the thought of leaving her to that sociopath ate him up internally.

He could feel Laurence's eyes on him, but chose to plant his head between his legs, resting his elbows on his knees.

All he wanted to do was feel Aimee in his arms again, safe from the world around them. But he couldn't even do that right now.

"I've never seen you like this…" Laurence suddenly said.

Chilian quickly wiped away the tears forming in his eye and sat upright. "I guess she means more to me than anything ever has…"

Laurence sighed.

Awkward silence was rare between them. But it was bound to happen sometimes, and this was one of those times.

The quietness was eating him alive and he wanted out. Wanted to run away and hide. But if he left now, his anger would only continue to simmer under the surface, and probably spill out over some poor servant.

"What do I do…?" he asked with a trembling voice. Laurence was clearly taken aback by the heavy question, but remained silent as he thought of an answer that wouldn't hurt Chilian's feelings too badly.

"I would say, nothing… Go take over my lesson and let some steam off. Continue visiting her, make her feel better I guess…"

"I can't do that, and you know it…"

"Then do something else."

"Like what?"

"Take the throne! At this point it might be the only way."

Laurence shook his head in vain and started inspecting his broken blade, but without his knowledge he had planted an idea in Chilian's head.

"You're right…" he said slowly, while thinking everything over in his head.

"Wait, what—"

"I'll do it."

Laurence looked horrified. "Chilian, it was a joke, don't take it seriously—"

"Think about it!" Chilian stood up and started walking around as his brain went into fifth gear. "My dad always wanted me to pursue the throne, and Maxim clearly isn't a proper fit for it. He doesn't care about the responsibility and takes all the perks for granted. His majesty has always wanted me on the throne above Maxim, and I already have his favor, so maybe if I can convince him of making me the next ruler... I would have full control of Maxim and I could keep Aimee safe..., I could give her a good life..."

His mind was going a hundred miles an hour, and the adrenaline rushing through his veins only made his thoughts more insane.

"Chilian, this is dangerous to discuss out here in the open, and it's not that simple!"

"Of course, it's not simple! This is gonna be the most complicated thing I've ever done. More complicated than trying to talk my father out of marriage arrangements."

"But Chilian, there's a reason you turned down the idea."

Chilian thought about it for a moment. His father had before tried to get him to win the throne for the family. But he had denied it not wanting neither the responsibility nor the rivalry with his cousin. Chilian knew that he would be leaving the country in incompetent hands, but he had made up his mind back then.

But the more he thought about it the more it made sense in his fussy head. He had always known that if Maxim came to power, Oplia's citizens would suffer from poor leadership. He would drive the economy into pieces with his wicked parties and leave everyone in poverty.

He could stop that. Save thousands of lives and have Aimee live comfortably on the countryside as she wished. She would be safe, and he would have the power to keep it that way.

But what if she didn't want that? What if she wanted something he couldn't give her? He had to talk to her about it and get her opinion. And then if she agreed he would go straight to his parents and tell them about the matter.

The adrenaline picked up and the blood was rushing through him faster and faster as he conducted the plan in his mind.

"Chilian!" He turned around in a frantic movement to see Laurence's conflicted eyes. "This is the highest form of treason, and you know it. If people found out we would both be dead by morning, and I don't want any part of that." Laurence stood up and walked over to him, standing as his equal and his oldest friend.

"You came to me years ago. You told me that you wanted a free life, without power or responsibility. You don't want the crown. Don't throw away everything for the sake of a single girl. For now think it over and wait. Maxim quickly gets bored of his toys right? This will probably be the same thing, so wait it out… Okay? Don't do something you will regret down the line."

His firm hand on Chilian's shoulder felt reassuring. Grounding. His breath calmed down and the adrenaline disappeared.

What was he thinking? He couldn't take the crown from Maxim. He had spent so many years shaking off the responsibility of it all. He couldn't just go back on it from one day to the next.

He sighed.

"Give it a week or two. If you still think it's a good idea, discuss it with Aldrick." And just like that Laurence walked away, leaving Chilian more confused and split than ever before.

Chapter 10

A Poet for an Escort

"Doll... Wake up..."

Aimee felt a gentle hand slowly stroking her forehead. Her eyes were heavy, as she opened them to see what was going on.

Although she wished she had stayed put, as she saw Maxim's chillingly warm smile, sitting over her.

"There she is. Did you sleep well?" he asked quietly.

"Your High—" she stopped before the mistake was made. "Maxim...?" she whispered, terrified. "What are you doing here...?

"Shhh... Did you sleep well?" he asked instead of answering her question.

He was still stroking her head, almost lovingly, and the longer it went on the sicker she felt.

She nodded carefully, not sure where the conversation was going. She was far too tired to deal with this right now.

"Good..." His smile was even sweeter now, and the sight was oddly alien to her. "Yesterday when we were standing together, you just fell asleep." He laughed at the thought. The sound sent shivers down her spine. "So I took you to bed. I guess yesterday was a bit much, am I right?"

Aimee nodded again, unsure.

His smile widened.

Then a disturbing thought struck her. She turned her head to look at the other side of the bed and sure enough all the silky sheets were ruffled, and a silhouette of a head was visible on the pillow next to hers. Terrified, she looked back at the smiling prince.

She hadn't noticed before, but his usually so perfect white hair was even more messy than yesterday, and he was wearing the same white unbuttoned shirt and black pants.

"Did you sleep here...?" she asked carefully, clearly trembling.

Maxim moved his hand from her forehead to her cheek and gently stroked it as he admired her. "It was too late to walk back across the hall, and besides, I wanted to make sure my doll was settling in well here," he said quietly. "Are you?"

Aimee thought for a bit. She started looking around the room trying to come up with an honest answer that wouldn't anger him.

"I do like it..." she started hesitantly. "But... I'm sad..."

Maxim grinned confused. "Sad? What could you be sad about?" he asked, clearly not understanding what was going through her head.

Aimee took the risky chance and continued, "It's just... Are you really gonna keep me here? In this room, locked up like an animal?" she asked. She knew this was dangerous and that one sentence could send her to the palace's dungeons or maybe worse. "Well if I let her out, my little porcelain doll might fall and break. I don't want that," he whispered quietly into her ear, "so it's better to keep you here, where you're safe and within my reach," he said cheerfully. Aimee thought again. There must've been something that could convince him.

"What if... I had an escort," she said, "then I could go freely around and come to visit you while you work."

"No."

Aimee felt her heart sink down to her stomach. He continued: "I don't want you alone with some man. I don't even trust my own guards to walk me down the stairs." He laughed. "Absolutely not."

"What if it was someone that wouldn't do anything? Like…" Her head was spinning trying to find someone suitable. "What about Chilian?" she finally said.

Maxim looked suspicious. "Chilian, my cousin?" he asked, his face slowly turning sinister and hateful.

She had to smooth things out. *What was it Chilian had said about their past?* "Y-Yes! We kind of grew up together. He's practically my brother" She lied.

The thought of Chilian as a brother made her stomach turn, but she couldn't show it. *Or maybe it was the hunger?* "I trust him with my life and know he would never do anything bad to me."

She smiled sweetly at her capturer, who was still thinking it over. She had to give him something in return. She couldn't just ask him this without making it a good deal for him. "I'll never ask for anything again." She promised. "I'll come visit you every day, and we can go out on walks together in your breaktime," she said.

She could see that he was thinking it over and she couldn't believe it when he nodded. "Fine. I'll think about it. But only because I'm in a good mood." He stood up from the bed and started walking across to the door. When he opened it Lilly, Linari, Sheldy and some other maids came rushing in and lined up in front of him.

"Get her ready in about an hour and send her to me when you're done. Give her the shady blue dress. The one with the sleeves, you know," he said in a completely unfaced voice. Like he was a completely different person than he was just seconds ago. It scared her how fast he could change his personality.

"I'll leave you to them, doll. And in the meantime I'll think about your request," he said.

She couldn't help but feel thankful for his consideration, but it disturbed her deeply. He was the reason she had no freedom in the first place. It shouldn't be up to him where she could and couldn't go. So she let out a faint "Thank you." And waited till he had left the room to get out of bed.

The maids quickly swarmed her like small worker bees for their queen and led her to the bathroom where they drew a bath for her. The water smelled like vanilla, and small rose petals were floating around on the surface.

After the bath her maids did her hair up with a big sapphire pin, and began on her makeup. Not a lot, but enough to look normal and pretty. She noticed how they put extra product on her cheek that Maxim had slapped the night before. *Was it still red?*

Linari went into the walk-in closet that was bigger than the bathroom and came out with a beautiful misty blue dress.

The front ended just above the feet and continued around the back where it touched the floor in an almost veil-like appearance.

Wonderful light fabric made out the airy sleeves Maxim had talked about, and the chest was covered in a pretty pattern of white and gray gems.

The bodice was a little tight when she put it on, but otherwise it was a nice fit. The fabric used was light, and the skirt fell nicely around her. As for shoes, the maids had picked out a white pair of heels that went well with the blue.

As she looked at herself in the mirror she admired how pretty she was, but was quickly reminded of what the dress symbolized.

A pretty jail uniform picked out by her capturer, purely to

entertain him. And the wonderfully luxurious room was her cell.

In an instant the admiration of the person in the mirror turned to a poisonous burning in her stomach, giving her a terrible feeling.

And she then regretted thinking about her stomach, because suddenly she again realized how hungry she was. The last two days all she had had was a few sugar cubes and some fruits, and in the long run that wasn't enough to satisfy her hunger.

She cursed Maxim for torturing her like this and turned away from the mirror's reflection. The maids were quietly standing behind her awaiting her approval.

She smiled warmly to the girls in appreciation. A wave of relief left the maids and she couldn't help but feel grateful for having them.

Especially Lilly.

Since they arrived together, she had stepped up and showed how good of a leader she could be, when it came to the other servants.

She had been forced along to a foreign palace and had left her family back in Leirath to take care of Aimee. She was grateful to have such a loyal servant with her.

She sighed and looked at Sheldy, her head maid. She was older than the others by about ten years and was pretty muscular. Her hair was blond and her skin had a red tint to it. And then two bright blue eyes. She was very beautiful.

"Sheldy, would you please inform his Highness that I'm ready?"

She bowed deeply at the request and showed how graceful she could move her muscles.

Then she was gone out of the door and Aimee was left alone with the remaining four maids.

*

He had stopped for a moment. Hesitated.

His heart was pounding wild, and he had trouble controlling his breath. On the training grounds this was usually easy to control, but the thought of meeting the snake on the other side, was both terrifying and enraging.

He stretched out his hand and knocked on the massive wooden door. It was engraved with gold all around the frame and silver lined out a pattern showcasing the royal family crest. A giant blue and golden serpent wrapping around a delicate rose.

The irony was sickening.

The golden handle turned with a distinct click and the door opened smoothly to a sparsely lit office. It was very big with giant bookshelves and windows.

The room was neatly organized with books on one side and a workstation on the other. The marble floor was clearly new, still shining, and expensive paintings lined the wall. Although you wouldn't see them in the darkness.

Giant blue curtains blocked out the morning sun and left only candles to handle the lighting.

"Cousin, there you are," a friendly voice said in a little too happy of a voice.

He wasn't at the desk where Chilian would expect Maxim to sit. No, rather, he was standing over by one of the giant bookshelves, reading.

Chilian bowed his head. "You called for me, your Highness," he mumbled quietly. It was hard hiding the hatred he held towards Maxim, but he still tried his best to seem unreachable.

"You no doubt know my new toy, do you not?"

Chilian looked confused. "I'm sorry, Highness, your what?"

Maxim looked a little disappointed by his denseness, closed the book, and placed it on an empty space on the shelf.

"Well, you displayed quite the concern for her at yesterday's spectacle, so I would think you had some recollection of her," he said warmly. Chilian finally understood what he was talking about, and he wanted to rip out his tongue for speaking about her like that.

Maxim walked over the new floor to his desk, where he lazily leaned up against it. He probably rarely used it.

"Yes, I do remember that," Chilian mumbled trying to hold back the murderous undertone of his voice.

"Good, very good," Maxim continued, "well. I had a little conversation with her this morning, and she expressed her desire to freely roam the palace grounds. So she could get some fresh air and come visit me during the day, that is. Isn't that nice?" he said with that oh so classic smile of his.

Chilian pulled on all his strength for a response. "Yes, very nice, your Highness. But I don't see what that has to do with me?"

Maxim shrugged his shoulders and stood up from the desk. He walked over towards the window and pulled the curtain slightly aside. He looked out over the courtyard beneath him and paused for a moment.

He looked like he was in some kind of trance, staring down upon the servants running around like little ants. That's probably how he viewed them. Small insignificant bugs, which only needed to follow orders.

A smug sigh left his mouth and he turned to stare at Chilian again.

"Well the thing is, I don't want her going out alone, I mean, what if she tries anything? Something stupid..." he said in a disturbing humorous tone, "so I want you to guard her as an escort, and make sure she doesn't... attempt... anything. If you get what I'm saying."

A sudden rush went through Chilian. *What was Maxim thinking? He couldn't possibly be that stupid as to let them be alone together.*

Chilian took a deep breath.

"I would gladly take the position," he said trying to hold back the confusion clouding his voice.

Maxim sized him up for a brief moment, looking a little hesitant. But he gave in and walked over to him. "You will meet every morning at nine, and escort her to either the library, the great dining hall, or the gardens. If she wishes to stay in her room, you will be free to leave until she calls for you again. She will be back in her room latest at eight and every day you will take her to me at seven. Is it understood?"

Disgust went through his veins like poison. The thought of having to bring her to Maxim every day was sickening, but if he wanted to see her freely, this was the only option. "Yes, your Highness," he murmured quietly.

The prince was quiet for a moment.

"Shaz," he said referring to his personal maid, who was stashed away in a corner, "go and fetch my doll for me," he said.

The maid bowed deeply, but Chilian was pleased to see the hatred on her face when she stood up again.

She quickly ran out of the door and left the two men alone. Maxim had turned around to pour something clear into a golden cup, and turned to ask, "Would you like a glass of gin? Or wine perhaps?"

Chilian was surprised that his cousin was drinking straight

gin in the morning but decided on the wine, so as to not seem rude. They shared a small toast together which in itself was a rarity. But alone and without a greater company, an almost unheard of act. They had never spent time together as children, and when they were forced to be in each other's company it was either in the king's Advisors Hall or at a family dinner.

The atmosphere was clearly awkward, and the silence was suffocating as Chilian poured down the wine.

It was very sweet.

A knock at the door almost sent him choking, as he turned around frantically. He heard Maxim's cold laugh behind him, in a clearly mocking tone and felt a tad embarrassed.

"Come in!" Maxim yelled at the people on the other side of the door and placed down his golden glass of gin.

The door slowly opened and in the frame a small shadow appeared. The figure looked around for a short moment before carefully sliding into the room.

Aimee looked beautiful in the misty blue dress. She had almost a ghostly appearance as the light fabric surrounded her silhouette.

She was looking tired and the makeup her maids had applied couldn't hide the bags under eyes. But the shining turquoise gems were still as bright as ever.

She quickly bowed to Maxim and when she stood up again her eyes widened in surprise as she saw Chilian smiling subtly at her. A quick smile of her own flashed over her lips, but she quickly snapped out of it and turned to the prince again.

"Maxim..." she said quietly. Chilian felt his body burning as he realized what he was making Aimee do. The anger over the humiliation Maxim was putting her through grew to an inferno.

Maxim, however, looked pleased by her performance. "Doll,

come here," He said and a shiver went through Chilian as the order was given. But she complied and started walking towards the smiling maniac.

"Yes?" she asked sweetly and yet timid.

"I have considered your request and have decided to give you this gift," he said.

Her eyes lit up and the bags under them were hidden by her enormous smile. She looked so beautiful, when she smiled like that. Chilian couldn't help but feel his knees soften a bit at the sight of her glowing expression.

Maxim continued, "You will be allowed in certain areas of the palace and the gardens, and you will report to me every day. But Chilian will tell you more about this later. You are both free to go," he said.

Aimee happily glanced up at Chilian and in return he gave her a reassuring smile. They both bowed before Maxim and were on their way out when he stopped them again.

"Doll," he said quietly. Maxim then started walking over toward her and without warning planted a kiss on her forehead. "Thanks for last night…"

Chilian felt a knife go straight through his heart.

The words strung together to a knot that blocked his throat and the flow of air. He forced himself to put up a cold façade, but really, he was screaming. Maxim was probably trying to provoke him and the best he could do was try and look unfaced by it.

Aimee stood nailed to the ground scared of even turning away from his cousin, and Chilian could see from a distance how much she was shaking. She slowly bowed her head and left the room, leaving Chilian and Maxim alone. He slowly glanced over at the prince and saw him slowly downing the last of his gin. A single drop missed the targeted mouth and slowly made its way down his chin.

He put down the glass but didn't get to say anything before Chilian stormed out of the room. He was fuming, red as a tomato and felt like hitting something. Or someone. Actually just Maxim.

When he came out of the room and found himself in the hallway, he quickly looked around to find Aimee.

He caught a glimpse of the blue fabric disappearing behind the door to her chambers, followed by a group of maids walking out.

Chilian hurried over but hesitated before the door. He overcame the sudden fear, knocked quickly, and opened it.

"Blossom?"

He stepped into the brightly lit room and took a moment to look around.

Even before the door had closed behind them, Aimee jumped at him laughing her heart out, and clinging to his neck. Chilian was unprepared for this and briefly lost his balance. They swayed around and almost fell down before he again found his footing.

"Whoa there, what's going on?" he asked, before returning the embrace by wrapping his arms around her waist.

She looked up at him, with tears in her eyes and the biggest smile he could imagine.

"I can't believe he agreed, I simply can't!" she said with her head buried in his chest still laughing like a child.

"Yeah! About that. *What the hell is going on?* What did you do? And what in the world happened yesterday after I left?" he asked aggressively, "you owe me a big explanation."

Chilian tried to sound angry, but he couldn't help it and got swept away in the happiness in that moment. He laughed along, picked her up by the waist, and started spinning around while their laughter filled the giant blue room.

After a while they slowed down and Chilian placed her down gently. "Now tell me," he said with his arms still holding onto her, "what the hell happened?"

"Okay, yes of course..."

She suddenly stopped herself from speaking and her stare became distant. All happiness was drained from her face as fast as it had appeared and was replaced with a numb, almost disgusted expression. She crossed her arms as if she had gotten cold all of a sudden. She tried stepping away, but Chilian had already started worrying.

"What is it? You can tell me."

She looked up at him, with an expression that was hard to distinguish. "This morning I woke up with Maxim beside me... He slept beside me without my knowledge."

"He what?" Chilian said, his teeth grinding against each other as he spoke.

"Yes, it happened and now it's over, thankfully."

Chilian couldn't help but see red. He tried looking as neutral as possible, but it was clear from her sorry eyes that he was clearly angry. "Well, we got to talking and I asked to have an escort so I could walk around the palace. I said what you told me about our summer together and that you were like a brother to me!" She laughed. "He ate it raw and now here we are."

Chilian was too stunned to speak. The rollercoaster of emotions he was experiencing was starting to make him dizzy. But the only thing he could think of was Maxim's enormous stupidity. A smile planted itself on him again and he couldn't help but absolutely adore her.

He moved his hand from her waist to her cheeks and leaned

in to tell her, "You're a fucking genius!"

He leaned in even further and kissed her forehead. Aimee placed her hands on his, and laughed along with Chilian, tears running down her cheeks over the small victory.

He loved her so much.

"What's that?"

Chilian turned around in a frantic manner. "Bl-Blossom? What are you doing here?" he asked while trying to hide the paper in his pocket.

Aimee was standing at the door, looking at him with a tilted head. Her light blue summer dress looked nice on her with the embroidered stars and moons along the lace hem. She looked tiny between the giant puff-sleeves, and it didn't help that she looked absolutely adorable with her hair tied in a bow on the back of her head and the pink curls running hanging down her shoulders.

She started to walk towards the bed and with a little difficulty made her way on top of it to sit next to him.

"So?" she asked, "Gonna tell me or not?"

"No!" Chilian tried to avoid eye contact, by staring down into the bedcovers. But Aimee moved into his vision by laying down in front of him.

"Please tell me," she said while getting more and more impatient. "I promise not to tell anyone," she said with a smile.

Chilian hesitated. But then reached into his pocket and pulled out the now crumbled letter.

"Here..." he said while handing it over. The second she took it he slid down the giant bed and laid down on the floor in embarrassment.

***

Aimee opened the letter, curious as to what was so embarrassing.

Chilian's handwritten letters made out four short sentences, on the white surface.

Hair as pink as berries.
Eyes as green as seas.
Mind as sweet as flowers.
But temper red as apples.

"It's embarrassing, I know." She heard him say. His voice was muffled by him hiding his face with his hands. He was all curled up and Aimee couldn't help but find it sweet.

"Chili?" she asked softly, "is this about me?" Some faint mumble-like noises seemed to come from him, but nothing understandable. "Well, I really hope this isn't about my grandfather," she teased, referring to her mother's father.

Chilian jumped up, disgusted even by the thought of it. "OF COURSE NOT, WHY WOULD I EVER—"

He didn't get to finish. He stopped dead in his tracks as she leaned in.

Aimee slowly removed her lips from his cheek again and watched his entire face turn as red as her hair.

"I love it," she said with a smile. She jumped down from the bed, handed Chilian the letter back and walked towards the door again. "I'm going to the pond to play; would you like to join me?" she asked.

But Chilian didn't reply. He stared at her with eyes of disbelief, not really sure if the kiss was real or if he was just in some sort of wonderful dream.

Aimee let out a faint laugh at the sight and walked out of the room again. But as she walked down the hall, she heard the running footsteps behind her, and knew her prince was right behind her.

Chapter 11

Swords and Roses

Aimee couldn't help but almost drag him along as she walked through the halls of Withall Keep.

She was too excited to breathe the fresh air outside to walk with grace and she simply hoped that no one would notice her eagerness.

"Aimee, for heaven's sake slow down! You'll get in trouble with the guards!" She heard Chilian warn behind her, but she didn't care. She wanted to get out of that cage, wanted to see the outside again. And wanted to feel the wind in her hair.

They made it down the stairs to the main hall, onwards to the left and over to the giant glass gates. The doormen barely opened them before she jumped out into the little freedom she had.

Even though it had only been a few days, since Maxim had taken her basic human rights away, it had felt like weeks since she had strolled down the glowing white stones making up the paths, lined on either side by newly cut fresh grass. The summer sun felt welcoming on her pale skin and the light breeze running through her hair tickled her sensitive skin.

The blue sky looked astonishing, and she was blinded when the palace's white surface and golden roof met her eyes. She was so overwhelmed that she briefly tripped over her own feet.

Chilian quickly snapped her back to her senses as he held her upright and prevented a collision with the ground. She felt the embarrassment rise to her ears.

"A little excited are we?" he said with a smirk. She liked when he smiled like that, and she appreciated that he didn't seem to mind her childlike behavior.

"I'm sorry. If you were being held captive by a maniac of a prince, wouldn't you be happy to get away from him too?" she whispered fully aware of all of the guards and servants around them, no doubt snooping in their conversation.

Chilian held back a small laughter and winked at her. "Well yes, I can see the appeal to running around like a four-year-old stumbling over her own feet," he teased.

"Oh shut up, you're just an escort," she mocked, and saw his expression turning 'sour' over the insult.

"I'll have you know, young lady, that I still technically have a higher rank than you, and that when this is all over you'll be in much trouble for looking down upon me," he said.

"Hey, I thought you said you didn't like your rank."

"I didn't. I said I didn't like the formalities. Entirely different."

She smiled, grateful to have him by her side. To support her. And protect her best as he could.

She thought back to the day on the staircase when he confronted all those soldiers, and was hit in the head with a sword, knocking him to the ground. And how he had yelled at Maxim afterwards. How he had sneaked into her room, through the maid's stairway and how he without hesitation had suggested a plan to get her out of there, even though it would have been a certain death sentence for him.

"Thank you," she said, a little teary.

Chilian looked as if he had understood her thought and gave her a saddened smile in return. "Remember, I got you. And I'll make sure you make it out of this, okay?" he said reassuringly.

A sudden image flashed before her eyes. Clouded at first, but the more she thought about it the clearer the picture got.

It was the pond back at home. A boy was sitting by her side. Blue eyes. With a soft voice.

"...You got me too..."

She looked up at Chilian again. He was still giving her that reassuring smile. She looked over at the guards standing by the white columns holding up the palace's walls.

Out of the corner of her eye she saw Chilian's expression change to a concerned look.

"Princess, what's wrong?" he asked. The pet name set her back a little.

She was disoriented. Her stomach felt empty. The sun kept burning her eyes, and she was dizzy.

She felt her eyes tearing up again. Chilian was now looking concerned at her.

The image of the boy flickered again.

"Aimee, are you all right?" Chilian asked now looking really worried. He placed both of his hands on her arms and shook her a little, trying to reestablish a connection. Everything caved in at once. It was so overwhelming.

She was so hungry.

And confused.

The sun was scorching.

"I'm sorry..." she whispered mostly to herself. Everything darkened a little. Her legs felt weak. Her head was too heavy. She could feel a cold sweat breaking out all over her body. Suddenly, her right foot couldn't keep up the balance any more, and she fell through the warm summer air. Everything slowed down as black and white flickered across her eyes.

But instead of meeting the stone path beneath her, she felt two strong hands around her, and she was stopped midair.

She heard the other guards around them reacting to her sudden collapse, but Chilian was quick. "Stay at your posts, this doesn't concern you!" he yelled in a sharp authoritarian voice and continued, "okay Aimee, you're scaring me here. You have to sit down, so forgive me for this."

She didn't know what he meant, and barely had any recollection of anything, so she almost didn't notice when something swooped her off the ground and carried her away from the entrance to the main hall.

She was on the edge of passing out in Chilian's arms as he walked her over to a nearby bench. She felt safe as she was laying there in his arms, so close to him.

He gently placed her down and went on his knees on the ground beside her.

"Okay, just take a moment, and breathe. Can you hear me? Breathe. Slowly," he whispered. He was holding her hand, gently squeezing it while trying to keep her awake. She followed his instructions best she could, with only half her conscience available, and slowly got a hold of herself. She figured that the sudden fatigue she felt was built up from everything that had happened. So many emotions, so many changes, and the lack of food coming her way. She hadn't processed it all properly yet and it had clearly been tearing on her, without anyone noticing.

The darkness around her vision slowly disappeared and all she was left staring at was the pretty blue sky, and its fluffy white inhabitants.

"I'm sorry…" she repeated.

"Don't apologize for anything, just breathe, just… focus." She heard Chilian say next to her ear.

"Okay..." she responded, happy to have him by her side.

Her head was now cleared, and she could see straight again. She turned her head to look at Chilian and he was a little closer than she had first expected.

She could almost feel his breath on her chin. She felt a slight red tint spread across her nose.

"Are you all right now?" he asked while looking extremely worried.

She sat up straight on the bench and tried to take in everything that had just happened. She had a few times before experienced this phenomenon. It started happening when she was a girl. She had been deadly ill and the doctor had prescribed a questionable kind of medicine. She was given it unknowingly and it had for a long time rendered her with phases of fatigue, dizziness, and even amnesia.

She had never fully recovered from it and the stress she had received these past few days must have triggered it again.

She looked down at Chilian.

He was on one knee in front of her still clutching her hand. It was dangerous to do so in public, cause people could very easily mistake the situation.

"Thank you, but if you don't have any intentions of proposing, I suggest you get up," she whispered, wary of the guards nearby.

Chilian's face turned suspiciously red, and he stood up immediately. She couldn't help but let out a soft laugh as he awkwardly positioned himself beside her as a proper guard. She was still dizzy, and the laughing only made it worse, but it was okay.

There was silence between them for a bit.

"Thank you," she said softly.

"Does it happen often?" he asked in response. She thought about it.

"It's gotten better over the years."

"And are you all right now?" he then asked. She looked up at him, as he turned to look down at her. She smiled bravely, trying to convince the both of them that she was doing better. He still looked worried. "I would like you to see a doctor. Just to make sure—"

"And what do you think Maxim would say when the doctor tells him I fainted on your first watch?" she asked, trying to lighten up the mood with a dark joke.

It helped and Chilian let out a small chuckle. "Yeah, you're right, that would probably be the end of this whole thing... So. How do you like the outside today? I ordered especially warm sunshine for you," he joked while still keeping a wary eye on her. Aimee's smile widened and she felt the dizziness almost completely disappear.

"Yes I noticed, and it is greatly appreciated. I've missed the outside."

"It's only been a few days though?"

"You try and stay in there in constant fear then."

He was silent after that.

She quietly closed her eyes. Felt the warm sun touch down on her skin and spread a tingling feeling across her shoulders and face. A small gush of wind rushed through her hair and as the leaves in the trees leading down the small road rustled, she felt at ease once again.

Chilian's voice suddenly joined the peaceful moment. "Are you all right again?" he asked, still worried. He was standing with his hands behind his back, mimicking the soldiers standing along the walls.

"Yes, I'm fine now. I was just overwhelmed." She went silent for a moment as she thought to herself. "You train with the guards right?" she asked.

He seemed a little unprepared for the question but nodded shortly. "As I've said, I was knighted two years ago, after having trained with the others. I was then assigned as trainer for the rookies. I've helped train many of the young men you see around the palace," he explained proudly. Aimee smiled to herself.

"Are we near the training grounds?" she asked curiously. He squinted his eyes in her direction, thinking it over with himself.

"It's a bit far. I don't think you should walk that distance."

She frowned. "What do you mean? I am perfectly capable of not falling on my face every five steps, thank you."

"Well as you just demonstrated so elegantly, clearly not."

She had the audacity to stick out her tongue in a childish tease and stood up. "Come on old man, I don't want to just sit around, and look pretty."

She then promptly lifted up her skirt and started walking down the white pathway.

She heard Chilian following behind her and turned her head to see a slightly concerned face.

She sent him a faint reassuring smile and let him catch up to her.

They walked side by side down stone stairs, passing rosy flower gardens, tall bushes, and a small group of ladies having tea.

Aimee had never participated much in those kinds of activities. Only a few times when her father's political friends had visited with their daughters. It was always awkward, so she ignored them, and they ignored her. They continued down a graveled road to a less fancy part of the garden. A big yard of sand was filled with training-dummies made of hay, swords and other weapons on wooden racks, training facilities like running tracks, archery courses, paddocks and stables for horses, and an unlimited supply of training equipment. Men were out in groups led by various knights and warriors she knew from her studies back home.

"I still don't understand why you would want to come here. It smells and it's dirty, and most of these men probably won't like you very much. Or maybe they'll like you too much..." he mumbled realizing how many potential threats could appear there.

She shrugged it off and walked over to a fence, overlooking a small group of people learning spear throwing. Their instructor was Sir Colyn Aquil, older brother to her sister's fiancé Archduke Maulus Aquil. Colyn had passed the title on to his much younger brother and had become the king's loyal servant instead. They had never met, but she was well aware of him.

His long black dreadlocks were tied back in a big ponytail, and as he demonstrated the techniques with the spear, they moved over his broad shoulders like rope being tossed around on a ship.

In a sudden turn he spotted the two of them by the fence and gave Chilian a strange look. Colyn said his last instructions, and quickly ran towards them, leaving the young men looking confused and unsure of where to aim the long pieces of wood.

As he got closer she noticed his strangely light-blue eyes and the small gap between his smiling teeth. He looked friendlier than a child's teddy bear.

"What's this, Chili, got a lady on, finally?" he asked in a teasing manner, while Chilian and Aimee's faces started to burn bright red.

Chilian was just about to protest the embarrassing question, but Colyn cut him off. He gently took her hand and planted a light kiss on its back. "What in the world would the Archduke's daughter be doing all the way down here with us dirty men?" he asked her with a smile.

"You know who I am?" she asked, stunned at his fun and forthcoming way of being.

"Well we are soon to be family, so it is only fair to know you by heart. And I couldn't overlook the hair."

Aimee felt her ears burning by the obvious sign of her heritage.

Chilian moved around uncomfortably and joined in on their conversation. "Hold up, family? I'm sorry, but I'm not quite sure if I follow—" he said confused.

Colyn laughed loudly at the poor man's confusion and took Aimee's hand once again. "Well didn't you know? We are to be married next month."

For a split second Chilian's eyes went dark, and his face turned white as his jaw dropped to the floor. But then he realized Colyn's smug smile and looked at his friend with tired eyes. "Haha, yes very funny. What's actually going on here?" he asked, more annoyed than she had seen him in a long time.

Colyn laughed again and had to dry tears from his eyes as he did so.

"His brother is marrying my sister soon, so we'll be siblings-in-law," she explained, while quietly laughing along with Colyn.

Chilian still didn't seem very amused by his friend's joke but looked more relieved than before. She met his gaze, and he shared a small smile with her.

"Honestly, I feel sorry for your sister. My brother, Aquil, is probably the dullest man you'll find out there. And let's just say he isn't really fond of women, I'm afraid."

"What do you mean by that?" Aimee asked curiously. Colyn glanced over atChilian who was now sharing his troubled look. They both knew something she didn't.

Chilian cleared his throat. "Aquil doesn't particularly find comfort in women's company. He much prefers that of mens. There is of course nothing wrong in it, except the fact that he is to be married soon…"

Aimee finally realized what he meant, for the first time in her life pettied her sister a little

"So what, are you coming to the wedding, my Lady?"

She thought about it for a while, before coming to the conclusion. "I'm afraid I'm not invited," she said with a timid chuckle. The laughter died out around her, and she felt the air around her shifting to a heavier atmosphere. Colyn leaned in over the fence that was dividing them and let out a slight sigh.

"So you're the black sheep too, I presume?"

She nodded slightly and felt a gentle hand from Chilian rest on her shoulder in a reassuring gesture.

"Yeah, me too. After I gave up the title of archduke, for something as low as an instructor at the royal palace, I've been like a thorn in their eye," Colyn explained with tired blue eyes.

A moment of silence went by as they reflected on the words just spoken, until Colyn broke the heavy silence once again.

"So, what actually brought you two here?" he asked, trying to change the subject.

Chilian took the lead.

"Well, this lovely lady dragged me all the way down here after randomly passing out in the gardens. I have no explanation for it, so I was actually hoping for one."

He walked over in front of her and leaned up against the

fence next to Colyn, clearly anticipating an answer.

"I just wanted to see where you spend most of your days, that's all," she explained. Once again she saw Chilian's cheeks turn a slight pink, but he shrugged it off quickly.

"This isn't a place for someone like you, M'Lady. You'll get hurt, and then we'll both be in trouble," he said, obviously referring to the cold bastard lurking around somewhere in the palace behind them.

She was a bit insulted by the lack of trust he had in her abilities, and she made a face that spelled it out rather clearly. She could see him realize what he had just said, and the slight pink on his cheeks disappeared, leaving only an expression that told her he regretted his words. Deeply.

Colyn laughed again at the show they were putting on, and she laughed along with him, although Chilian still looked regrettably embarrassed.

"What do you say we give the Lady a little demonstration, huh?" Colyn asked when he had regained his breath, "a little sparring match like old times? You have been slacking off lately."

"A match? Right now?" Chilian asked stunned, "but what about your group?"

"They can manage without poking each other's eyes out for a little while longer. Besides, wasn't that the whole point of coming here, M'Lady? For a little action?" he asked with a glimpse in his eye. Her smile doubled in size and she looked over at Chilian who was waiting for her approval.

He then tossed his head back in an dramatically tired fashion. "Fine…"

"That's the spirit!" Colyn loudly said, gave Chilian a pat on the back, and walked a little away from the fence.

Chilian looked over at her with a warm smile. Then he buttoned down his blue velvet waistcoat he had been wearing all day, revealing the loosely sitting tunic underneath. Stunningly, Aimee noticed the small pearl hairpin she had given him, still attached to the collar of his shirt. She felt a load of butterflies releasing in her stomach, as he placed the blue waistcoat on the log fence.

Then he walked over to her and placed a hand on Aimee's shoulder. "May I?" he asked mysteriously.

With a skeptical smile she answered, "Yes." He moved his hand to her waist and with the other scooped her off the ground as he had done before.

She frantically threw her arms around his neck in shock over the sudden disappearance of the ground beneath her, and she received nothing but a giggle from her carrier. Slowly he walked her over to the log fence, swung her legs and skirt around to the other side and placed her down gently on the waistcoat so that her dress wouldn't be dirty.

When she had found her balance again he gave her the sweetest smile she had ever seen. He then athletically jumped the fence, like he had done it thousands of times before and landed in front of her.

He gently took her hand in his, and bowed deeply. "This victory is for the Lady Aimee Achillea!" he said loud enough for Colyn to hear.

"Yeah, yeah, don't get ahead of yourself!" he shouted back, while he was warming up his arms.

Aimee laughed at their fun banter, as Chilian stood up straight and kissed her hand. She felt her blood rushing through her veins as his lips left her skin and he looked up at her with a mischievous smile and a glimpse in his eyes. Then he winked at her and turned around to face his opponent.

*

They had done this many times before. Colyn was no doubt bigger than him, but Chilian knew all his tricks and techniques, so he didn't fear much. The only problem was the fact that Aimee was watching him, and his every move. He knew it would be embarrassing to lose in front of her, and that this fear could be his downfall.

He reached down and took out the sword that his uncle had bestowed upon him the day he was knighted.

The green emerald shined on the handle, and the relatively simple blade was screaming to taste the steel of another sword.

Colyn also took out his own sword, a little more accessorized, but still modest. He had that grin he always had just before battle, so Chilian knew this was going to be fun.

He felt the pearl on his tunic touch against his collarbone and he felt thankful for the small gift that gave him so much strength.

The men started circling each other as was routine, waiting for the other person to initiate the fight.

Now and again his eyes flashed over towards Aimee, sitting on the fence overlooking everything. She looked so out of place in the purple dress she was wearing, surrounded by haybales and equipment. And the red hair following the wind's movement made her look almost mystical in the bright sun.

He almost didn't think the thought through before Colyn lunged his sword towards Chilian's right leg.

A gasp was heard over from the fence and Chilian barely managed to block the attack. Blade against blade met in a song of steel and he felt the hit quivering in his bones.

He had become distracted, and Colyn had happily taken advantage of this grave mistake.

Colyn subtracted his sword to prepare another blow, but Chilian was quick to duck as the sword again flung through the air, this time toward his neck.

Chilian stood up again, his feet firmly planted in the ground, and sat off in a lunge toward Colyn. Steel against steel sung in quick succession, their bodies moving and avoiding ongoing attacks like a dance to the melody of battle. They danced in circles and squares, jumping out of the way and responding swiftly with counter attacks.

They could go on for an eternity. Chilian remembered their longest fight that had lasted more than two hours. So he decided that as not to hold up Aimee for too long, he would have to end this quickly.

He thought of multiple ways to disarm his friend but concluded that he would try and use his size against him.

So he waited for an opening to appear and there it was.

Colyn was swinging his sword in an angle from the right and had left a narrow space under his arm. Chilian took the opening, and recklessly jumped toward the sword. Time stood almost still as he just barely avoided the blade coming down from over him. He took a swift dive and landed behind the giant man.

There he was in a perfect position to kick his opponent's knee joint, forcing him down on one knee and leaving him baffled. Chilian stood up again, quickly took a strong grab around his ponytail, and pulled back to expose Colyn's neck to his blade.

"Do you surrender?" he asked as he was trying to regain his breath.

"Where the hell did you learn that move?" was Colyn's only response. Chilian laughed at his bewildered friend and helped him to his feet again.

As they were finding their footing again, they heard Aimee clapping from the fence. She jumped down and hurried over to them.

"That was incredible!" she said, as Chilian was brushing off some of the sand that had stuck to him in the dive. "Are any of you hurt or—"

Colyn gave her a warm smile. "Don't worry, my little Lady. I trained this bastard myself, so if he had gotten hurt, he would have been sleazy, and I would have dunked him one for it."

"Yeah, because beating them are apparently the best way to teach children," Chilian said annoyed, while wiping away some sweat from his forehead.

They all laughed although he sounded a little more bitter than the other two.

They all walked over to the fence again, where Aimee dusted off the waistcoat that she had been sitting on and gave it back.

"So tell me already. What's the deal between you two? Cause I've never seen you show interest in any woman," Colyn blurted out without a second thought behind it.

Chilian could feel himself hesitating as to answer, and so it seems Aimee did. Colyn picked up on this, quicker than Chilian would have liked. "I'm uh... her bodyguard..." he hesitatingly answered.

Colyn looked at him with a skeptically raised eyebrow. "Yeah, and I'm the queen," He said plainly.

Aimee thankfully took over the conversation, and answered the question in a believable way.

"You see, we're, uhm... old friends and when I arrived here in the capital, Chilian was assigned to watch over me. So I don't run around causing havoc everywhere." she laughed.

But Colyn still seemed skeptical and with a mischievous look proceeded to drop the biggest bombshell of Chilian's life.

"Well, it's an excellent cover for you being lovers," he said nonchalantly.

Chilian felt his blood both leave all parts of his body and rush all throughout it at the same time. His jaw dropped to what felt like the floor, and he was blinded by both the embarrassment, rage, and also, unexplainably, a little relief.

Aimee was also completely flustered by the sudden remark. Her face was almost as red as her hair, and she was having difficulties saying anything other than non-connecting sounds. All while this was going on, Colyn was laughing his ass off at their reaction.

"We are certainly not—" Chilian couldn't even finish the sentence, without his blood almost boiling over. This only made Colyn laugh even louder, and Chilian regrettably started noticing the people throwing spears looking.

So Chilian grabbed Aimee's hand. "Come on, I won't expose you to this idiocy any longer."

She said nothing as he almost dragged her back towards the main gardens, in hopes of escaping the situation.

"Tell me how it was tomorrow!" He heard Colyn yelling behind them.

Chilian turned around in a blink of an eye. "YOU SHUT YOUR MOUTH, OLD MAN!"

He felt his ears burning. Colyn was still cackling as they moved further and further away from him, and finally they reached the flower gardens. Chilian was so upset that he kept dragging Aimee along the bushes of roses, as red as his face.

But a small chuckle broke through the rushing sound of blood running a hundred miles an hour through his veins. Aimee had stopped and was now both laughing and crying at the same time.

Her hair was messy, and some of the makeup she had on was running a bit as tears rolled down her cheeks.

She looked hilarious. The situation was hilarious. And he couldn't help but join her in the ridiculous laughter.

Chapter 12

A Snakes Bite

They both finally cooled down, but she couldn't stop smiling at the absurd conversation they had just had.

Chilian was still holding her hand firmly as if he had no intention of ever letting go.

"I am *so* sorry, Aimee. Tomorrow I'll teach him some proper manners," he said while gesturing to his sword. Her smile widened.

"Oh, I hope I'll get to talk to him some more, he was so fun and energetic!" she explained joyfully.

"No way in hell I'm letting him near you ever again. It's bad enough I see his stupid face every day. You shouldn't have to suffer like that." She chuckled again.

"So what's all this about him being your teacher?" Aimee asked and started walking down the path they were on.

"Well, I met him when he was about nineteen. He has largely stayed that age for our entire friendship. Then I started training with him and my friend, Laurence, when we were both nine. Later me and Colyn entered the king's council at the same time. He was a little bitter about that."

"How old were you?"

"Seventeen, I think?"

"Seventeen? I wasn't even allowed outside my father's

residence at seventeen." She admitted, flabbergasted, "How unfair!"

They both thought about the differences in their lives. It was quite weird for her to imagine people of her own age doing such important things as counseling *the king,* but she figured that she had been very sheltered for most of her life. It only made sense she couldn't really believe it.

A silence arose.

"That night…" she started, unsure of how to proceed, "you told me about our so-called past." She felt Chilian stiffen a little beside her. "And I think I'm in a state where I can handle it," she said while looking out over the flowers next to them.

"Aimee, that's still too early…"

"No." She stopped. He turned around to look at her, sporting a concerned expression. "I don't like being kept from the truth, Chilian, and you know something about me that even I don't," she said to him, "please tell me at least a little bit."

He bit his lip. Almost drawing blood. He didn't like the subject, that was clear. But what had been going on between them? And why did he remember when she didn't? Did it have anything to do with the amnesia she suffered?

He didn't even get to speak before the maid Shaz came running up to them. Maxim's servant. Aimee felt Chilian's hand tighten around her own.

"Sir Chilian? A message from his Highness," she explained and handed him a small piece of paper.

He looked over at Aimee with a concerned look and returned his attention to the small note.

He read it swiftly, and the light in his eyes slowly died down, as his expression changed to a mix of annoyance and hate.

He handed her the small paper. "The prince requests your

presence. Immediately..." She took the paper and read the short message on it.

Deliver my doll to my office. Hurry.
– Maxim

She felt her stomach turn. All color draining from her face. Her body freezing up.

She had forgotten about the daily visits he had required as he had always canceled unexplainably.

"This way, my Lady," Shaz almost whispered.

"No!"

Chilian's sudden outburst shook her to the core. Shaz looked terrified. Who wouldn't be scared after working for Maxim.

"I'll take her there myself. Go take a break," he ordered sharply, while looking around rapidly, not focusing on anything in particular.

"But His Highness said—"

"Go! Now," He sounded angry now.

Shaz shook at the command, but hurried back through the gardens. Chilian continued looking around, until his eyes locked in on something specific.

"There," he said and grabbed her wrist. Without any notice he started running and Aimee was forced to follow along.

"What are you doing? This isn't the way to his office! Stop!" she shouted at him, but he didn't seem to notice, as he dragged her along into the small forest at the foot of the walls surrounding the palace. Her feet were already hurting in the high heels and the corset made it hard to breathe as she desperately tried to stop him.

She was already dizzy like she had earlier and she was afraid of falling over again.

"Chilian, *STOP!*" she shouted, hoping she would break through to him. And that she did. He stopped running and turned around to face her. But she wasn't prepared for the distressed expression that had colored his entire face gray. The teary eyes filled with pain. The cold hands he placed on the back of her neck. She had expected anger, but he looked scared. Terrified.

"Listen to me, Aimee. I'm not letting him near you, okay? I'm not doing that!" His voice was shaking. "There's a small gate through here that's rarely used. I'll take you through there outside. I'll find a horse and I'll take you to Stillgate. My family is there, they'll protect you. I'm not taking you back to him, I'm not doing that!"

He sounded angry, sad, and frightened all at the same time. It was enough to make her teary too. But she couldn't. She couldn't leave. Couldn't leave the monster without bringing everyone else in danger.

She took a deep breath.

"Listen to me. You'll be killed if we do this. Our families will be killed if we do this. Everyone we know will be tortured. I can't do that. I can't have that on my conscience. I have to go back," she said as calmly as her trembling voice would allow her.

"I won't let you," he whispered. She felt his hands shaking behind her neck.

She was unsure of what to do. She wanted to leap into the air, throw herself around his neck and let him take her away from this awful place. Wanted him to stick to his word and take her away against her better judgment.

But she reached up behind her neck and held his two trembling hands.

"Please stay outside the door…" she whispered. Quivering

at the thought of being left completely at the prince's mercy.

He let go of her neck and put his arms down his sides, in what looked to be agonizing despair.

She gave him a smile and took a deep breath. His hair was all messy again, and he had a little sand up over the small scar running down the left side of his face. The blue eyes were still as warm as ever.

Incredible, how two sets of eyes could feel so different when they were looking at you. One pair was kind and loving. The other only saw you as a meal. The flame in her heart grew a little by the warm feeling he was giving her.

He still looked miserable. And scared.

But she didn't have time to comfort him.

She turned around and started walking back towards the original path they were on. She didn't give him a chance to make a choice on her behalf. This was her decision, and he could only abide by it.

And shortly after she heard heavy steps following her trail.

The sound of the wood against her knuckles echoed throughout the empty corridor. It was like the sound traveled all through her body, from her hands to her toes and up in her ears where it rung like a loud bell.

She felt Chilian standing next to her. He was still on edge. And she couldn't blame him one bit.

No way back... she mumbled to herself. She heard Chilian clenching his hand by the small remark. She was just happy they weren't on the run right now, like he had wanted them to do earlier.

Her thoughts were suddenly punctured by the click of the golden handle that opened the giant door in front of them.

They cautiously stepped into the dimly lit room. All air left her lungs as she saw the pearly white hair glimmering in the faint sun, penetrating parts of the drawn curtains. He was sitting over behind his desk.

Maxim was wearing a tight sitting blue waistcoat with golden embroidery, outside of a white tunic. He looked the part of a prince, that was for sure.

She curtsied deeply so as to not anger him. But Chilian still stood sturdy as a mountain.

"Ahh, finally. That took some time did it not? I thought I said to hurry?" Maxim said with a smooth, yet slithery voice.

"I apologize, your Highness. I'm afraid we were on the other side of the gardens, when your message reached us," Chilian said in a composed voice.

Maxim's face briefly changed to that of dissatisfaction, before returning to the almost cheerful expression.

"All right, that is of course understandable. Another time though, hurry. I've missed my little plaything..." Maxim said in an almost childlike tone.

"Of course, Your Highness..." Chilian growled in a low tone.

Maxim sighed before dismissing the maid in the corner. Not Shaz but another one. They hadn't noticed her, but it was probably her who opened the door before. And as quick as a mouse, she was gone out of the door. *Good thinking,* Aimee thought to herself.

"Oh, Chilian. I heard you had a council meeting at this time right? You'd better go as well." Maxim spun.

Aimee's heart dropped again by the thought of being left alone with him again. But she had chosen it, so there was nothing to do about it.

In the corner of her eye, she could see Chilian hesitating. But at last, with a bitter expression, he nodded his head in Maxim's direction, and turned around. They made eye contact one last time before he disappeared, out of the door.

And she was alone with the beast.

She cleared her throat. "You called, your High… I mean… Maxim…?" she almost whispered, as she felt the cold sweat forming on her back.

He looked displeased by the stumble in her words but said nothing. Then the ominous smile formed on his lips again. It was wider than normal. She felt her stomach turn.

Without a word he stood up and slowly made his way over to her. As a vulture, he started circling her, waiting for her to either talk or make a mistake, so he could bite into her frightened skin.

"How did your dress get so dirty?" he asked out of the blue.

She was taken a little aback by the random question but managed not to show it too much. "I visited the gardens today. I suppose the grounds are quite dry and dusty in this warm weather," Aimee said quietly. She had kept her eyes on the floor and saw Maxim's boots still circling around her.

He sighed. "A shame. Next time, try and keep it clean. It fits you so well."

"Of course, Maxim…" The word felt like venom burning through her tongue. She wished she could spit it back in his face.

He stopped in front of her. "Look at me," he demanded.

Aimee lifted her head and saw the damning smile, plastered over his face.

"Are you hungry, my doll?" he asked casually.

"A little, but it's manageable," she lied.

The smile widened. "Are you sure? I would hardly call a

little fruit and sugar cubes a proper meal."

"Well, I am all right," she simply answered, wanting no trouble.

He sighed at her boring answers. That was a good thing perhaps. If she was too boring and no fun at all, he would get tired of her and let her go.

The plan started forming in her head. But as it did, she briefly lost connection to the real world and the actual danger she was standing in. And Maxim took the opportunity.

As a true snake he snatched out with his hand, roughly grabbing her jaw. Again.

And once again she was taken aback by the sudden and painful movement that rendered her almost powerless, with the overstriking fear.

But Maxim was still as calm as ever, grinning at the sight of her wild, fear-induced eyes. She felt like a dog at a kennel being inspected by their future owner, and not being able to do anything but surrender to his will.

She hated him.

With the hand he wasn't holding her still with, Maxim reached behind her head and pulled out the blue gemstone pin that had been holding her hair in a loose bun all of this time.

Bright rosy-red hair fell over her shoulders, tickling the exposed skin all around her neck. The flaming locks formed a curtain over her right eye, partially shielding her from Maxim's satisfied smile.

He threw the gemstone pin across the room, shattering it to a thousand pieces, as it hit the newly polished floor. A hand ran through the red curtain in front of her revealing the rest of the maniacal smile in front of her.

Goosebumps formed down her spine and arms as the cold

fingers slowly glided through her silky fire.

"You're so beautiful, doll..." he whispered quietly. He sounded almost entranced by her. His hands tightened around Aimee's jaw.

"*It hurts... let go*," she whispered back, through her clenched teeth. But her plea for mercy was met by nothing, but an eerie silence. The blue eyes came closer. She couldn't move. Couldn't escape.

The eyes closed.

She tasted venom. Cold and slithering lips, packed to the brim with what felt like a thousand needles piercing through her skin. She tried to move. Tried to escape. But he held onto her.

She felt the tears roll down her cheeks. And then the pain shot through her lower lip as his teeth sank into the thin pink skin. Warm blood started dripping down her chin. She wanted to scream. Struggle. Fight him.

A fire started inside of her. A little flame that slowly grew. And for every second his lips laid hers, the flame burned bigger and brighter. A storm was brewing inside of her. A storm of hate and anger.

She promised herself that she would make him pay. Make him bleed too. One day she would pay him back for everything. And he would regret this moment, more than any other wrongdoing he had ever done.

She swore on it.

She would remember this moment. *She would make him bleed.*

*

The door closed behind her.

The blood was still dripping from her chin. The tears in her eyes had dried, and left her cheeks annoyed by the remaining salt. She had never seen clearer than right then.

"Aimee!"

Chilian suddenly appeared in front of her, with a terrified expression, making it clear to her how worried he was.

He started inspecting the wound on her lip, and his eyes went dark. Murderous. "What did he do? How?" he whispered.

She said nothing.

That was apparently enough to send him off the rails, as he reached for his sword and was about to storm through the massive doors. But Aimee quickly placed herself between him and the entrance, blocking his way.

He looked shocked by her action but stood back. She sighed. "I'm tired. Can you take me to my room?"

The wilderness in his eyes calmed down and left him, looking more confused than ever. She wondered what he was thinking in that moment. Maybe he was thinking of that escape plan again. It would suit him. Or maybe he was just planning on how to twist his sword in Maxim's stomach, to cause the most pain.

She started walking away from the door, followed shortly after by Chilian's comforting footsteps. It was first there she realized how weak her legs felt. Her jaw was aching, and the blood, still dripping from her lip was slowly coloring the purple dress magenta. The wound was apparently deeper than she thought as it continued to soak her dress down the hall. She needed to be cleaned up and that quickly.

They finally reached the doors to her chambers. The two guards that were posted outside of her door gave her concerned looks as she passed by them, but she ignored them and entered the room, with Chilian following close behind her.

Inside, Linari and Lilly were talking quietly while cleaning off some of the bookshelves in the main entrance.

As they both heard the doors close behind Chilian, they turned around to bow deeply, but one look at Aimee's condition was enough to have both their jaws drop.

Lilly looked completely terrified, as the blood only continued dripping down her chin. There was no doubt that Aimee looked a little morbid.

"Please, leave us," she demanded in a stern voice. She didn't like talking like that, but she had nothing reserved for politeness at that point.

"We should clean you up first before anything," Lilly said, clearly concerned about her employer. She rushed over and was about to start wiping her chin, but Aimee had had enough.

"Leave!" she said again. She felt bad for the poor maid who was only trying to help her, but she didn't have the energy to care for her feelings right now.

The clearly shocked maid bowed quietly and rushed to the door. Linari followed close behind her and closed the doors behind them. Aimee and Chilian were alone again.

She let out a faint sigh as the silence placed itself around her like a comforting blanket. She could feel the blood slowly breaking through the dress's fabric and decided that she would have to change and clean up the mess she was making everywhere.

"Wait here, while I go wash this off," she said with her back still turned to Chilian.

"Afterwards, we need to talk," he said, in a concerned voice.

She turned her head to look at him. He was staring at her, with a mix of despair and anger covering the usually kind and warm eyes. *How could he and Maxim ever be related?* She couldn't understand it, and she probably never would.

She managed to send him a small smile before she turned around again and walked out into the cold bathroom.

The girl that met her in the mirror looked nothing less than terrific. She was pale. The blood had been smeared out over her chin, and she had giant red marks left behind by Maxim's slimy fingers. Her messy hair was sticking to her face and her eyes were red after having cried earlier. The faint make-up she had worn today had run down her cheeks along with her tears and had exposed the giant dark bags under her eyes. She looked nothing like herself.

Aimee quickly washed her face, took off the now magenta dress and threw it on the ground. She took a brush through her hair and put on the bathrobe that was hanging from a shelf. It was red and went down to her feet. It felt like a thin, but warm silk.

She took one of the small cloths from the sink, dipped it in some cold water and placed it on the wound in hopes of the bleeding stopping.

When she was done she felt the hunger starting to manifest inside of her again. *Annoying,* she thought quietly to herself.

When she left the bathroom she felt refreshed, but also extremely tired. It must have been the nerves that had been in play the last hour or so.

She looked around the room to try and spot Chilian. He was sitting on the floor with his head on his knee and holding his sword so hard it must have hurt his hand.

She walked over to him, not saying a word.

Aimee sat down in front of him.

"I'm sorry," he whispered. His voice was trembling, in a mix of fear and anger. She didn't like that. She took his hand. Chilian lifted his head to look at her. His hair was as much of a mess as it was earlier, and she couldn't help but find his angry eyes endearing.

"It's not your job to protect me," she said. He looked at her confused. Aimee took a deep breath. "But I can't do it myself either… When I was in there… without you. I was completely vulnerable. And I hated that. I want to be stronger, Chilian. I want to defend myself… I don't want to be useless any more," she explained. She was determined now. To be stronger. To be more capable. She was no longer the little girl who arrived at the palace just a few days ago. She had to pick up the fight somehow.

He looked at her, not sure of where she was going with it all.

She sighed. "If you wish to help me, then teach me to fight back. So I can help myself, and not leave everything to you. Teach me like you teach your guards, and make sure, I'll be all right on my own."

Chilian said nothing.

He looked conflicted. He had probably never heard such a request from any of the women in the palace. They had the guards to protect them. They didn't have to fight for anything.

"Aimee, I couldn't possibly teach a noblewoman to fight."

"Why not?" she asked, "Chilian, if you're always so worried about me then why not make sure I can stand my ground?"

He looked lost. His hand was warm in hers.

Moments went by in silence, as they were both sinking in despair. One thinking every possibility over, and the other waiting for confirmation. "It isn't a good idea…" he said quietly.

"Well, it's the only idea right now," she said in a stern voice. She wouldn't give up on this, she just couldn't.

He was clearly in another place, and she felt like she couldn't reach him. He was thinking of something else, and she knew what it was.

"If I tell you what happened in there, do you think you would change your mind?" she asked.

"I have a pretty good idea of what happened already..." Chilian spit out through his grinding teeth.

"Good! Then help me!" Aimee demanded. She felt her blood boil as she placed her hands on each side of his head and forced him to look at her and her wounded lip. "This is what he did to me. Because I am weak and unable to do anything against him. Help me, please!" She felt her body burning by the rage Maxim had ignited inside of her. She had never been angry or spiteful before, but what he had done was the last straw. She was over the edge now.

Chilian seemed to notice the flames in her eyes. The passion and burning anger was spreading from her, engulfing them both in an inferno, set alight by Maxim.

A fire fueled by rage and the need for justice and revenge. She saw the spark in his blue eyes light up even brighter than her own.

"Okay... I'll teach you," he whispered.

She felt a happiness flood in over her, as his warm, blue eyes smiled at her with the support of what felt like a thousand armies.

She leaned in toward him and gave herself the luxury of feeling calm as he cradled her in his arms.

It felt so familiar.

"Aimee!"

Her door flew open, and the light from the hallway blinded her for a little while. The shadow ran towards her over the carpeted floor and jumped up into her bed right beside her. "Hey, what's wrong, I heard a scream," Chilian said concerned, as he checked if she was hurt anywhere.

"Nightmare…" she whined, still trembling.

Chilian had paused for a minute, not quite sure of how to comfort her. He sighed shortly.

Then he climbed down next to her under the covers and wrapped his arms around her. Pulling her in close to him. She was still shaking all over her body, but his warm presence felt nice. Safe.

"What was it about?" he asked in a calming voice.

"A snake… in the field outside," she whispered, having somewhat gained control again.

"I'm sorry…" he mumbled into her hair.

They didn't say anything else. Slowly sleep took over again, and they dozed off in each other's arms. Safe from any snakes in the fields.

Chapter 13

A King, a Princess, and Two Princes

"Okay, are you ready?" he asked.

She finished tying her hair up behind her head in a tight bun and put the golden brush down on the table. They were in the big office in her quarters and had cleared a pretty spacious area for their training. Chilian had lend her a small uniform used by the up-and-coming knights on the training grounds. It was a somewhat nice fitting pair of green pants and a beige tunic that was tucked in and tightened around the wrists with leather strings.

Chilian was wearing his usual white shirt, black pants, and knee-high boots. He had taken off both his sword and waist coat and was warming up his arms. Attached to the neckline of his shirt was the little pearl pin she had gifted him that fateful night. It gave her a little rush every time she saw it.

He was now making sure the two carpets he had stacked on top of each other would be soft enough to land on.

It had been a few days after the incident at Maxim's office. Luckily, he hadn't called for her ever since, and sometimes he had even sent Sheldy up with a little food for her.

She was both happy and scared about not seeing him. It only broadened the chance of something bad happening soon.

"I'm ready," she said.

"Right..." He looked concentrated as he made sure the last things were in place for them to begin. It was exciting to see him at work, she thought.

"So. I'm only gonna teach you techniques with the intention of deflecting, not really harming. Because if you suddenly break the prince's arm, I'm sure he'll want to have a word with you afterwards." Chilian tried to joke.

"Yes, of course."

"We're gonna start off with some simple things, like stance, balance, and movement. Later on we'll put you in one of those big dresses, so it'll be more realistic."

She nodded.

"So first off. I'm gonna have to pull your hair for this, is that okay?" he asked and stepped over behind her and waited for her approval. She nodded. "All right, I'm gonna grab your hair now." She felt his hand fasten around her tight bun. "Now I'm gonna need you to spread your legs a little and bow down in your knees." She did as he said and was now standing in a kind of awkward, light squat. She could feel him right behind her, and noticed his light breath touching the back of her neck. She felt blood rushing to her ears. "Okay, and now hold on to my hand, and force your head under my arm." She did as he told her and suddenly she was standing with his twisted arm, having him leaned over and forced him to let go of her hair.

"See? There you go," he said as he stood up again, "then the second you're free you run away. Don't give him time to go after you, understand?" he asked in a surprisingly strict voice.

"Yes, of course."

He smiled at her shortly. "All right, again."

A little over an hour had passed by. In this time she had twisted almost all of Chilian's limbs, kicked him to the ground multiple times and at one point had him flying over her back, to land on the carpet.

"Oh my goodness, are you okay?" she asked as she felt Chilian fall to the floor a little harder than other times. She hurried down by his side as he laid completely still, apparently tired after their session.

"Yeah, yeah, don't worry, I'm used to this. Just a little break. I think you could use one too." He laughed. He was right, she was exhausted.

Aimee smiled at the giant man and laid down beside him.

"You're surprisingly strong, you know that?" he asked.

"I'm pretty sure you went easy on me." Aimee laughed.

She looked over at him to see a guilty grin.

"Wanna hear something funny?" he asked.

"Sure," she answered while trying to catch her breath. But it was hard with the giant hole in her stomach that was usually filled with food. She was slowly getting used to the hunger, but the fatigue had sat in long ago.

"You're better at self-defense than my friend Laurence."

"Really?"

He nodded with a smile.

"What do you want to do after we're done?" Chilian asked.

She thought about it for a second.

"I think I'm just gonna relax here. I'm absolutely exhausted. What about you?"

"Well, I think I should get down on the training grounds again. Laurence and Colyn must surely be missing my expertise at this point." Chilian let out a slight laugh by the thought of them apparently having to take care of all of his chores, while he babysat her. She felt a bit embarrassed by that revelation but said nothing.

"How do you even make time for all of your other duties, when you have to be here with me?" she then asked.

There was a bit of silence as he thought about it.

"Well, I've moved all of my training sessions to after I leave here. Then I review some of the material from the days' meetings and send my own opinions in a letter."

She sat up on her elbows, as she thought it over. She realized that he was still keeping up with all of his other duties while attending to her. He was working himself to death. And it was all because of her. *How was he not sleep deprived? How was he still so focused when he was around her? So witty?*

And here she was throwing him around the room, demanding him to teach her self-defense.

She felt her airway slowly blocking up as her conscience slowly narrowed her mind.

She sat up, leaving him on the ground looking confused.

"I'm sorry I had no idea…" she mumbled as the guilt slowly crept in.

"What? There's nothing to be sorry about—"

He didn't get to finish because a knock was heard at the door to the office.

She sprung up and fear took over. They were doing all of this in secret. Chilian had said that the guards outside would ignore the noise cause he had ordered them to, *but maybe someone else had reported it to Maxim? Maybe he was coming to punish her again?*

Her frantic mind was interrupted as the knock sounded again.

She quietly tiptoed over the cold marble floor, trying to

avoid the mess of moved books and tables everywhere. She could hear Chilian grabbing his sword behind her and felt him following her over to the door. He hid over to the side, ready to strike down if any threat was to be on the other side of the door.

The person knocked a third time, and Aimee reached down for the golden handle. With her heart beating louder than normal, she opened the door to see nothing but Linari's kind smiling face.

"His Highness has asked me to deliver this to you," she said referring to a small envelope, on the silver platter in her hands.

The envelope was white with a familiar golden seal, staring up at her. A snake wrapping around a rose. Her capturers family sign.

"Thank you, go take a break," she said, as she picked up the rather luxurious paper. The girl's face lit up, and suddenly, she was gone again. Aimee closed the door behind her and went back into the office to open the envelope.

Inside a familiar handwriting greeted her.

To my dearest Doll,

You have been invited to my father's, King Aldrick Istatis', 13th anniversary on the throne. It will be here at the royal Withall Keep Palace on the 31st of June, where we are to celebrate him and his long and eventful reign.

The party will consist of a dance in the ballroom, followed by a grand feast afterwards in the great dining hall.

You will of course also be celebrated as my new favorite toy and will be a special part of the party.

You will arrive at the big ball room with me as an escort in the evening. I will personally pick you up at eight, so make sure to be ready. I have told your maids of the dress you will be

wearing, so just make sure you look your best.
From your own, Maxim Istatis.

Her stomach turned.

A feeling of wanting to puke suddenly arose, but she ignored it.

She could feel Chilian reading in over her shoulder and saw as he gently took the invitation from her hand, as he read it closer.

When he was done, he sat down in a nearby chair, his usually calm face looking troubled. "Bullshit," he mumbled.

"What does this mean?" she asked out into the room, not really directing it at anyone.

"I don't know…" he admitted. Unconsciously, Chilian reached for the pearl on his shirt and started fiddling with it. A little rush went through her as she realized that his hand reached for it in moments of concern.

But the rush didn't last for long, as the thought of having to spend an entire evening in Maxim's company, overshadowed it.

"This is tonight," Chilian said, with a hesitance in his voice. "I received the invitation last night, but I didn't know if he would wanna showcase you yet. And especially not at his father's celebration…"

"Showcase me?" she asked.

"Yeah. When he was smaller he would always bring his most prized possessions to balls and parties to show off to the other children. I thought he had grown out of that. He is truly just a spoiled brat at heart."

Chilian sounded irritated. But she didn't really care. What she cared about was the humiliation she was about to suffer. And the shame she would bring over the entirety of her family and Edenran. What kind of rumors would spawn after she is seen as the prince's escort? Would people think of her as a whore? Sleeping with the prince for power? Or would they think that she was trying to shame her family on purpose? What if the talk reached her father back in Leirath, then what would she do?

It was like the thoughts sucked out all of the warmth in her body. Chills started crawling down her spine and she could no longer feel her fingers. The tunic she was wearing suddenly felt extremely thin and she had to hold herself to find just the slightest hint of comfort left in her cold body.

But then she felt a thick shawl being wrapped around her shoulders, and a warm hand laid on her cheek. With the other hand, Chilian turned her around, so they stood face to face. Or face to chest was probably a better description.

"Listen to me, Blossom. It's very important, okay?" She nodded hesitantly, not sure where he was going. But the serious look in his eyes was enough for her to forget all about the cold. "It's already three in the afternoon, which means he'll be here in about five hours. That will give you lots of time to prepare, and revise any ideas for a good performance, cause that is all that he wants. A good performance. Being submissive and pretty. Give him that and I'm pretty sure he'll leave you mostly untouched. I'll be right behind you at all times, okay?"

It was a lot to digest at once, but she felt she got the most important points down. She nodded again, hesitantly, still a little lost as to what she was supposed to do at that time.

Something in his eyes changed as he was looking at her. They went from being seriously irritated at the entire situation to a softer expression. Remorseful. Pitiful.

She loved his blue eyes. They reminded her of someone. Someone far away, holding their arms open for her to be comforted by. But she hated the pity. She didn't want pity or remorse, or sorrow. It made her feel like a weak little girl who couldn't do anything. She had been that her entire life. She didn't want to be that any more. She didn't want him to see her that way.

She leaned in, no sounds at all, and rested her forehead against his chest. He didn't do anything to push her away. On the contrary, Chilian leaned his own head down and gently placed a kiss on the top of her head.

Aimee felt the warmth return to her face and body as he wrapped his arms around her and held her in his comforting embrace.

It didn't last long though, as he gently pulled her away again. "I'm gonna go now and get some things in order. Call on your maids, and make sure not to be alone. Just as a precaution. I'll meet you again here at around seven, before he comes, okay?" She nodded. She didn't feel like speaking.

He looked conflicted. Like he didn't want to leave her in the big apartment all alone.

But he grabbed his waistcoat and sword, and off he was out of the door, gone. He was free to do such a thing. It dawned on her that she wasn't.

*

He hurried down the hall almost tripping, trying to button up that darn waistcoat. He was still sweaty after the lesson, and his hair didn't want to behave at all.

He certainly got many weird looks from all the court members he passed along the corridor. He accidentally ran into Grand Duke Shanlor, who looked rather startled. He continued down the hall and finally arrived at the giant wooden door.

It was detailed with silver and gold, and the familiar crest, hanging over the frame, looked down on Chilian, giving him an odd feeling of despair.

A last attempt to set the hair somewhat presentable, and then he knocked.

The door quietly creaked open and a familiar face appeared in the frame.

"Ah, Sir Chilian. It's been a while," the elderly guard said with a warm voice. The man named Geron, had been a doorman here as long as Chilian could remember. Even as a child when he would come here to visit the office, Geron would stand inside ready to welcome him with the kind smile and white beard.

"Yes, it certainly has," Chilian responded, "but this is sadly urgent, so I have no time to chat like usual."

"Of course, my boy." Geron nodded in understanding and disappeared behind the door. He waited impatiently as the seconds slowly went by. Finally, the door flung up again and Geron gave him the approving nod.

"Thank you," Chilian said as he passed by him in the doorframe.

He entered the small corridor behind them, greeted the six guards lining the walls and made it to the final door. He opened it with a slight hesitation and entered the room on the other side.

It was nicely lit up by the giant windows lining the wall and greatly decorated with artworks, well-kept plants, maps, parchment, books, and other luxurious office supplies.

There in the middle of the room, at the great desk he used to play under, sat The White Knight.

The Archduke of Slemith, and king of Oplia.

Aldrick Istatis.

His uncle.

He was looking older than usual, pale, and almost sickly. The light blonde hair and beard had turned whiter than snow, and his belly had definitely grown too. But the kind eyes and warm smile remained the same.

He was no longer the great warrior king, Chilian had grown up knowing. But he still respected the old man beyond belief. And most importantly his moral compass.

Chilian bowed down deeply in respect of the man in front of him, and waited for Aldrick's approval.

"You still come here, bowing to me like I was a god. I will admit that it makes me feel grand down here behind my desk, but I have told you many times that there is no longer a need for it," the king said with a smile.

Chilian stood up again, with a small smirk having been planted on his lips against his will. "You are always keen on jokes, aren't you?" he said with a cheeky voice. The elderly man laughed with him, and it was truly a joy to listen too.

"Now, my boy," he said in a little more serious voice, "I haven't seen you here for weeks. You send your opinions on stately matters in letters, delivered by maids, and have taken over the evening training. In the day you are almost never seen and when you are, it is with a certain someone... Am I right?"

Chilian felt like he was being scolded, but he couldn't see where this was going, so he simply nodded, while trying to look unfaced.

The king took a breath.

"I've had some of my people do a little investigation. Lady Aimee Achilleas, daughter of Sir Renan and Alnor of Edenran, and official guest of my son. Am I right?" he stopped to have Chilian confirm his information.

He nodded hesitantly.

"So, may I ask why you have been pushing aside your work for this girl?"

A wave of silence washed over the room. Two seconds. Five seconds.

"The prince appointed me as her official escort," he announced after careful consideration.

"How so?" the king asked.

More silence.

He didn't want to badmouth the king's one and only son in front of him, but he couldn't really think of anything.

"We are old friends, your Majesty. During the siege, I stayed with her in Leirath. We were very close. So he saw it fit that I escort her." he explained hesitantly.

The White Knight looked him up and down, and at that time Chilian wished he could read minds.

"My boy, are you in love?" he then asked bluntly.

The question startled Chilian. But he wasn't speechless. He didn't feel his ears go red and he didn't feel the need to clarify that it wasn't the case. In fact, suddenly, he found a weird feeling of both relief and clearness in his messy mind.

He looked the king in the eyes. "I believe so…"

The king smiled.

"You have grown much since the siege. I'll have to thank her for finally making a man out of you," Aldrick said while smiling under the white beard, "but why have you suddenly come here?

Chilian was taken out of the relief he had felt just a moment ago and once again felt the weight of the situation upon his shoulders.

He had trouble finding the right words and didn't recall the exact reason he had come there in the first place. Was it to ask for help? To have Aimee taken away from Maxim? Did he want the king to stop the entire ball from accruing? His body started trembling. He had left Aimee and came straight here. But why?

Why was he there?

As he got further and further lost in thought, he didn't notice the king's all-knowing eyes piercing directly through him. Reading him, like an open book.

"It's about Maxim, is it not?" he asked.

Chilian was lost for words at this point. His mind was too much of a mess to make out a single coherent thought.

But between all of the noise running through his head, one thing kept screaming louder and louder. Like it was his own subconsciousness telling him that it was the only thing worthy of trying. So he gave in. His entire body went almost limb as he swept down onto his knees.

This was the only way, was the conclusion he reached.

Maybe she would hate him for this, but he didn't care any more.

He was trembling.

"Uncle... Maxim is keeping her against her will. She is a prisoner not a guest... And I can't do anything to protect her against his torture, with the position I stand with right now. You told me years ago that you considered me more suitable for the throne than Maxim. Back then I had no reason to want it. But now, with her at the mercy of *him*... I have every reason to fight. If there is still a chance for me, then please. It would be for the better of everyone, and you know it."

Silence.

Chilian didn't want to look up at the man about to decide his fate. He was too scared of whatever expression would meet him if he did. This was probably his only chance at ever saving them both and being able to keep her safe for the rest of her life. Sure, his uncle could order Maxim to release her, but there would come a day when Aldrick wouldn't be around any more. They would be at Maxim's mercy once again.

If his uncle refused him this, Aimee would never again know peace.

Heavy steps sounded throughout the quiet room, getting closer to him by every second. He felt his hands shake along the wooden floor, while awaiting the king's next words.

A gentle hand was placed on top of his head, slowly brushing through the dark brown mess he called his hair.

"Why didn't you come to me sooner?" his uncle asked in a soft voice, "you know I would have helped you."

"I was confused… Scared…" he whispered.

The king sighed deeply.

"It pains me to say, but my son has always been disturbed. Coldhearted, and untouched by others suffering. He has always found joy in pain and torture, and have never showed regard for anything, as far as I'm aware. I will never place him on the throne, for the fear of what he would do to my kingdom. Most people know that. You have always placed the kingdom first. You have always sacrificed whatever necessary to keep the people safe. So there was no doubt in my mind who should inherit the throne after me. I know that you want the freedom that comes along without this huge burden. But we're both aware that Oplia would be doomed without you to lead it. I was just waiting for you to change your mind, Chilian."

His eyes widened. He finally had the courage to look up at the man he had admired all his life. He had no words. The single tear that fell down his chin, said everything.

A happy smile formed on his uncle's lips as he went down

on his knee and hugged the young man. Chilian was too overwhelmed to do anything. What did this mean? Was he going to be king? What would happen to Maxim? Was Aimee safe, finally?King Aldrick pulled away and looked at Chilian. It was his own blue eyes that were staring at him with such love. It was Maxim's eyes, Sofeel's eyes and his mother's eyes too. The eyes of Oplia's rulers, passed down through generations. Within them a fire burned brighter than it had for years. The king was proud of him. Chilian knew it just by the look of him.

"I'll announce it today at the feast, after everyone has gathered. I'll have to tell Maxim beforehand, so he won't be informed at the same time as everyone else." The king stood up again and started going over some important documents on his desk. Chilian was still trying to take it all in.

"So... Is that it?" he asked, with a trembling voice, not quite sure if he was ready for what was going to happen.

"Yes," the king responded, "from this moment on, you are Crown Prince Chilian Malvaria. Future king of Oplia and Archduke of Stillgate. Maxim will still receive the title of Archduke of Slemith though. Taking everything from him would have never been fair." Aldrick smiled.

King?

Was it real? He didn't think it would ever be this easy to win a crown. He had gone his whole life bowing down to Maxim. Would that change now?

More than anything he wanted to go see Aimee. Hold her tight and never let go.

"Geron!" the king suddenly yelled, still going over the documents on his desk.

Not long after the door opened up to reveal the old doorman's kind face.

"Send word for Maxim, I need him here immediately."

Geron looked confused for a moment, probably over the fact that Chilian was kneeling down on the floor. but he didn't question it. "Right away, my Lord."

He was gone as fast as he had appeared.

"Now," the king said, "to the hardest part..."

Chilian had somewhat calmed down again. The sudden shift in his status had completely turned around his entire way of simply existing. He didn't feel like any of it was real. He wondered if it was all just a dream he would soon awaken from.

But it wasn't. And nothing made that clearer than Maxim's expression changing as King Aldrick gently told him the news.

He was completely drained of all color as the fact slowly seeped into his corrupted brain. At that moment Chilian was realizing how much he was taking away from his cousin.

He didn't know how he would describe the feeling that formed in his chest. But it definitely wasn't regret. Or remorse for that sake.

He deserves this, the little voice whispered in his mind. And as bad as it was, he couldn't help but agree with it.

Maxim broke the silence that had plagued the room.

"So is that how it is...? I am now nothing?" he asked, clenching his fist clearly holding back the obvious rage that was boiling under his skin.

"You will always be something, my boy. For instance, you will still remain the prince of Oplia, and you will gain the title of Archduke of Slemith, when I am gone," the king said with both calm, stern, and gentleness all at once, "but you are to stay far away from lady Aimee Achilleas. She will be accompanied by Chilian to the celebration tonight."

Maxim was still white as a sheet. But his eyes burned. Not like the kings had done earlier. Or like Aimee's had done after that day in the office. This fire was cold. Evil.

A smile appeared on his lips. But it looked weird. Twisted more than usual. His eyes were too wide, and the grin too big. He looked insane.

He quietly bowed his head. Turned around and left the room, without permission. Without hesitation. Without a sound.

Chilian had imagined him screaming his lungs out, destroying everything within arm's reach and maybe even draw his sword in blind rage like he would when he lost an argument as a child. He was expecting everything, but a quiet acceptance. But now he was gone, out of the door, and out of sight.

Chilian had taken everything from him, and he had nothing to say.

"You should go get ready for tonight, my boy. Your lady will be waiting I'm sure. I would like to meet the person that changed your mind." the king said. The thought of Aimee finally being free from this horrible place was overwhelming. But the thought of having taken the throne from Maxim was still greater than any other relief. To think he would be king.

He never wanted the crown, and he never had a reason to. Was it wrong of him to take the position for himself, just to protect one person? Could he really just do that?

All the thoughts were still too much for him, so he bowed to his uncle and excused himself to his own chambers.

He had a lot to process and not enough time to even take a proper breath.

*

The knock sent goosebumps down her spine.

Surprisingly, she knew exactly who it was before Princess Sofeel stepped through the door with her recognizable footsteps. She looked more and more like a goddess each time she saw her, Aimee thought, as the pale woman greeted her with a soft smile.

"I'll be right outside!" another woman yelled from the hall, helping Sofeel to a soft giggle.

Sheldy and Lilly had been in the middle of discussing her hair for the evening when she appeared out of seemingly nowhere.

Sofeel was wearing another gorgeous blue and golden dress, similar to her own, the one Maxim had picked out for her. But instead of light fabric and many layers making Aimee look like a flower with blue petals, Sofeel's dress looked heavy, with some sort of thick silk, making her figure look slick and slim. The bodes had a low ringed neckline and her sleeves were short and revealed most of her shoulders and arms. Thousands of tiny golden details made the dress come to life, and a small and simple necklace decorated her elegant neck. Her silver hair was sat up in a braided bun, and a golden crown sat proudly on her head. Her face looked almost natural without much makeup, and Aimee wondered how a human being could look so otherworldly beautiful. She was the epiphany of royal beauty.

Aimee felt a little shame when she started comparing herself to Sofeel. She knew that if she started, she would lose most of her own pride.

"How are you doing?" the fairytale princess asked in a gentle voice.

"What are you doing here, your Highness?" Aimee asked, confused as to her presence. It had been an entire week since her last visit, so Aimee had mostly forgotten about her and their little talk.

"I've heard you'll be attending today's celebration as Maxim's escort. How do you feel about that?" Sofeel asked as she quietly sat down on the chair, across from Aimee and the giant mirror she was staring at. The maids had slowly started setting her hair in an agreed style.

She hesitated for a minute, not really knowing how to respond to the princess's question.

"I believe I'm scared," she answered honestly.

"Why?" Sofeel looked at her with calm eyes, waiting for her answer.

She had difficulty finding the right words, as the many possible scenarios passed through her mind. Then she said, "I believe it is in my nature to fear the unknown."

Sofeel leaned forward in her chair while considering Aimee's words. Then she placed a warm hand on her lap, like a friend comforting her.

"*I* believe that there is so much more to your nature. You're a fighter. I saw it the day Maxim took you away. You're brave ,and courageous, and that's why you're still alive. You're resilient. That's why you can endure this," she whispered, "today you will walk side by side with Maxim, and let the world know that you are not afraid. But prepared to fight."

The acknowledgment from this brilliant woman in front of her almost brought Aimee to tears. She had never thought of herself as brave, or courageous. She was a girl, wrapped up in a game she didn't want to play. She didn't feel like any of those things Sofeel had just called her.

"Why are you on my side in all of this?" she asked, trying to keep her shaking voice calm. Sofeel let out a slight sigh.

"That boy has tortured me every day of my life. From the

day he took his first steps till today till in the future where he will find amusement in my life being sold off to the highest bidder."

"You're getting married?" Aimee asked, not sure if it was appropriate to ask.

"Let's just say it's in the process," she answered silently. "Maxim has never done anything but hurt me in this life. Torture and punishment were always the norms whenever our parents weren't around. So I've stayed quiet all these years out of fear. But now, seeing this happening to someone as innocent as you… It's simply awful."

Aimee saw tears slowly forming in the princess's eyes. To think how hopeless they both were, was frightening.

"Will you be there tonight? By my side?" Aimee asked, hoping to have Sofeel's support at least through the evening.

Her hand tightened around Aimee's leg as a reassuring 'yes'. They were in this together.

As friends.

As sisters.

Chapter 14

A Party or a Funeral?

The second knock came at exactly seven, like he had promised.

Sofeel had left a little while ago, so she looked forward to Chilian's comforting company.

Linari didn't even get to reach the door, before it flung open and Chilian stormed inside. She had no time to prepare, as he picked her off the chair she was sitting on and started swinging her around the room, laughing his heart out.

She heard her maids gasp as she swayed through the air in Chilian's arms, completely stunned by his obnoxious behavior.

"It's done! It's over!" he shouted at the top of his lungs, as if the whole world should hear it.

She regained some sort of control over her wild emotions and quickly told the maids to scatter, as it must have looked absolutely scandalous.

"Chilian, put me down!" she yelled to reach through to him. He understood her demand and gently put her down on the floor again.

She carefully used him as support while trying to regain balance in her shaking legs.

"What's going on?" she asked, still trembling by her sudden flight.

Without warning he took her face in his hands and kissed her forehead. When his lips left her skin the smile he had when he barged in, had faded to a tender smirk.

"You're free," he simply said.

Her blood went cold. Her heart stopped in the middle of the beat. "You killed him?"

He grinned at her terrified and confused look. "No, of course not. I went to the king and told him everything. He took away Maxim's title and power. You're free now."

It was like a bomb that went off inside of her. Everything was rushing around in her body, heat was spreading like a wildfire and the hope and happiness she had longed for, suddenly brushed up without warning.

She felt a smile growing on her lips. "Are you lying to me?" she asked just to be sure it wasn't a dream.

He simply shook his head, with a smile too big for his own damn face. A sudden thought struck her mind. A thought she honestly didn't want to be true, but she couldn't see another answer for it. "If Maxim isn't next in line any more... Then who is?"

Her fear was confirmed when his smile faded, and two tired eyes pierced through her soul. She felt her heart break a little as she realized what he had done for her sake. The happiness she had felt just a moment before faded along with her expression.

"Why would you do that...? For someone like me?" She couldn't breathe properly. It was like a knot had been tied around her throat, and she was slowly suffocating.

In her panic she saw someone in front of her. A boy.

He was looking at her like Chilian was. With a tired smile. His hair was dark brown. And his eyes. She knew them. Bluer than sapphires. Warm and comfortable. Reassuring. The boy spoke. But it was Chilian's voice she heard, "I'll give you everything."

She snapped back to the presence as Chilian finished the sentence.

Aimee was confused and heartbroken. She couldn't think of anything worse she could have done to him. He had told her about wanting his freedom in this life. And he had just sacrificed it for her own.

She couldn't think of anything else. She wanted to tell him to take it back. Let her suffer, as long as he was happy. She didn't want him taking on this burden for a girl who didn't even care to remember their so-called past together.

Tears formed quietly in her eyes. She could do nothing but lean closer and envelope him in her arms.

"You shouldn't have done that… Not for me…" she whimpered into his shoulder.

She felt Chilian's muscles tense as he probably realized what he had done, how he had signed away his future, as a free man.

"Anything for you…" he whispered in her ear "Will you go with me to the ball?"

"Of course…"

And together they both dwelled on this new revelation.

*

The entrance to the great hall looked extraordinary, just like the last time. Only now everything was decorated with golden Isatis flowers in celebration of the king's thirteenth anniversary.

She remembered her father and sister leaving the estate once a year to participate in the magnificent party, but she was never allowed to come with them. Her father explained that the constant presence of her mother's red hair would drive him insane. Elniba would always laugh as she got told no, although their father did hush her.

It had always been clear who the favorite was, but his daughters bullying each other in his presence was still too much for the Archduke.

They probably weren't here tonight. Her Father was probably still south for business and her sister was most likely preparing her wedding up in Oldea.

Chilian was by her side, arm in arm, as they walked down the hall towards the enormous doors to the ballroom.

In the heat of the moment, earlier when he had sent her flying, she hadn't had any time to take a proper look at his attire. He was wearing a long, white coat, with small golden details lining the back and his sides. The sleeves were baggy and made of shiny golden silk matching all of the beautiful embroidery. He was even wearing golden, knee-high boots, which she could only imagine to be uncomfortable and his hair was messy again after having picked her up and flung her around her chambers. But it had clearly been brushed back beforehand. The little scar running down his left eye was more prominent than usually, and his blue gems glittered with a wonderful spark.

But the thing that kept taking her breath away, every time she saw it, was the small white pearl attached to his collar. When she had handed him it the night of the masquerade, she had never imagined how much it would come to mean to him.

It gave her butterflies just looking at it.

His sword with the emerald at the end of the handle was tightly fastened by his side, and his tunic sat tight under the coat.

He was probably the most handsome man she knew. Aimee felt her cheeks turning red by the silly thought.

He suddenly leaned in closer to her, as they reached the massive doors to the ballroom.

"Because this is a more formal party than the masquerade, the royal family will enter together and open the ball with a dance. Behind my uncle and aunt comes my cousins and then me and my family. And I wish for you to accompany me, alongside the others. I'm sorry for not telling you sooner."

Now she felt the small blush in her cheeks turn into a burning sensation. He wanted her to walk alongside him, the royal family and his parents, in front of everyone. Everyone. That kind of gesture was almost the same as directly announcing to the world that they were lovers.

Was he serious?

She couldn't even tell. As they got closer she saw people standing in front of the closed doors. She was absolutely baffled as she realized the company she now found herself in.

King Aldrick Istatis, The White Knight, stood in the middle of the group in a handsomely fitted white suit, matching Chilian's. To his left stood the queen Alryn Istatis, the sister of Archduke Shanlor and the Mother of Maxim and Sofeel. The two of them stood to the queen's left and looked perfect with their matching hair and neatly fitted clothes.

She didn't look at Maxim. She physically couldn't. She was scared that the familiar smile would cut through her if she met his gaze. *Or maybe he was looking at her with murder in his eyes?* After Chilian took his entire destiny away from him for her sake, it would only make sense for him to want her dead.

She just moved on.

Next to the king stood a somewhat unfamiliar couple. The woman looked almost exactly like Sofeel with white hair, pale skin, and an elegant posture. The dark blue eyes were also present. The man beside her looked strict, with a scarred face. He had shimmering green eyes and dark brown and silky hair. He was the spitting image of his son, Chilian.

Archduke and Archduchess Renan and Difis Malvaria of Stillgate. Chilian's parents.

She almost felt more nervous about meeting them than the king and queen.

As they finally reached the small group, the chatter quietly ended. She and Chilian bowed deep before the king. "Congratulations on another good year, your Majesty," she said just as Chilian had suggested she should.

"So, you're the famous Pink Lady?" the king asked with a warm voice. He instantly gave her a feeling of calm and welcomeness. That was more than she had ever felt, even back in Leirath with her family.

"I suppose I have caused a bit of a ruckus, haven't I?" She nervously laughed while clenching Chilian's arm as if she was holding on for dear life. "I apologize…" she said sincerely while looking down.

"You have had nothing to do with any of this. It is my son who has completely violated, both you and your name. I know compensation probably won't solve his wrongdoings, but please, let me offer you a sum of twenty-five thousand, and a wish. You can ask for anything and I'll try my best to grant it," the king said with a regretful voice, clearly trying to make up for Maxim's actions.

For a moment she considered taking his offer, right then and there and ask for a carriage home. Away from this place. But out of the corner of her eye she saw Chilian. Waiting for an answer like everyone else. He had sacrificed everything for her. And she was thinking of leaving him. How could she be so selfish? She was a disgusting person, she thought to herself.

Aimee did some quick thinking.

"Your Majesty. I would like to save my wish for a later date. And as for the money, I have no use for it as I am well off already. Could I instead ask for it to be sent to a homeless shelter somewhere in the city? I feel it would be better off being used for someone with a bigger need than me."

Most of the men around her looked at each other with faces switching from confusion to disbelief.

But when she saw the approving expressions of Sofeel, the queen and Chilian's mother, it was more rewarding than any cash prize she could ever win. Even the king looked pleased with her decision, as he came to terms with it.

She felt a warm hand squeeze her arm gently and glanced up at Chilian who was looking at her with proud eyes.

"What a generous offer. You seem to have a heart of gold," Sir Renan said. She couldn't determine the tone of his voice. Either he was annoyed at her for refusing the king's offer, or else he truly admired her for sacrificing her personal gain.

"Thank you, Sir Renan, that is very kind of you," she replied. To her surprise, she saw his cheeks jerk back as if to simulate an odd smile. She brushed it off as a nice gesture.

"Now that everything is in order again," the king said, "let's make our entrance."

Everyone around him nodded in agreement and the long parade queued up to their given places. The king and queen in front, of course. Then their children, and afterwards the Malvaria's.

And in the very end was her and Chilian. The nerves she had tried to suppress the entire evening were now suddenly springing back up, nearly choking out all of the air in her lungs.

She quickly tucked Chilian's arm to get his attention. He looked over at her and she wished his gaze would calm her, but quite the opposite happened. She leaned up to his ear and whispered, "I've never done anything like this in public…"

It took a little while for him to register what she was saying, but when it did he smiled gently. "I've got you, okay. All of this is just a performance to keep the other nobles entertained. Just smile and follow my lead. I promise to help you if you get lost in it."

His words were so sincere. She couldn't think straight as he leaned in to rest his forehead on hers. He was so close, she could feel his breath. His eyes looked at her with such sincerity, she couldn't breathe.

She pulled away quickly. "Damn it, don't make my knee's buckle before the dance," she whispered.

Now it was him who turned red. A smile broke through her lips, as the gates opened before them. A massive crowd of nobles moved aside for the door and the royal melody started playing over the trumpets. Never had she been part of such an ordeal.

A loud cheer from the crowd was heard as the parade slowly started moving through the masses. She clung to Chilian's arm for dear life, so as not to be overwhelmed.

The giant hall was beautifully decorated with even more golden Isatis flowers and long, silky banners hung from the ceiling, in a dark blue color matching the families signature eyes.

Everyone standing around them was wearing luxurious looking dresses and suits lighting up the entire hall with their shiny crystals and jewelry. There were hair in every style, a million different shapes and sizes and the smell of expensive alcohol roamed among them all.

In the crowd she saw a few familiar faces, like Colyn Aquil, people she had passed a few times on her tours in the gardens, and even Grand Duke Shanlor who looked rather drunk already.

She also caught a glimpse of the Dahlian family, with the Archduchess Sonor and her two sons Laurence, and his older brother. She and Laurence had met once before in a corridor, but other than that she had no recollection of any of them.

She kept searching the ballroom a little while longer. For some reason she wished to see Elniba and her father there. Maybe to see both their jaws drop as she came parading in with the royal family? They could finally see that she wasn't worthless, like they had told her all of her life. But of course they weren't there.

Elniba was basically a prisoner in Oldea with her fiancé and her father probably still wasn't back from the south. She didn't really know how to feel about it. So she was just happy to have someone like Chilian by her side.

The crowd finally opened up to a big clearing in the middle of the room. The enormous chandelier in the ceiling looked fabulous, with the lit candles lighting up all of the crystal details around it. The floor looked newly polished with intricate patterns, carved out of the marble, and replaced with other colorful stones. There were five main illustrations making out the five duchies', head family crests.

In the middle was Slemith with the golden snake and rose. To the left was Edenran with Aimee's family's green sword and pickaxe, on the right was Oldea with the forests, and Stillgate and Cateron made up the north and south. Together they displayed how connected they were with golden thorns piercing out from Slemith binding them all together.

A beautiful illustration of Oplia and all the duchies within it.

She hadn't had time to admire it at the masquerade due to the constant dancing, but now, when Aldrick and Alryn, the king and queen walked in to stand in the middle of it all, she couldn't help but be awestruck by the sight.

Without a moment's notice the band started playing a wonderful melody she had heard Elniba play many times in her violin lessons. The king took his wife in his hands and together they started swaying around the floor in a dance described by many as magical. She now understood the term as it felt almost enchanting, watching the queen's purely white gown glide across the floor. The white and blonde hair swinging around each other and the red in the cheeks becoming more prominent as they danced their hearts out.

In that brief moment she felt the great love they shared. Their marriage was most likely arranged, but as they trusted one another with the eyes of hundreds upon them, they looked truly young and in love. Without even noticing she had started squeezing Chilian's hand as she tried regaining the breath she had lost as the king and queen had started the evening.

"Are you ready?" Chilian whispered as she realized that she was probably hurting him at that point.

"What dance is it?" she asked, still bewitched by the beautiful display in front of her.

"Just follow my lead, the show doesn't have to be pitch perfect."

"But we'll be the laughing stock of the year if it isn't…" she whispered, now reconnected with the real world.

Without any notice, Chilian gently turned her head, away from the king and queen, and toward his own.

"The only thing that matters to me is you, enjoying your freedom to the fullest. Nothing else is more important to me. So let me lead you in this and reassure you that no one else matters in this moment. It's just you and me."

The flame inside her grew as his words touched every corner of her heart. She reached up to his collar and took the pearl pin from him. He stood still as she raised it to her lips. Slight hints of red lipstick had stuck to its white surface as she smiled up at him. Gently, she placed it back onto his collar, just in time for their apparent cue.

Chilian took a few seconds to get his eyes off of her, and finally they followed his parents out onto the dancefloor. Smoothly, they started dancing in a circle around the royal couple. Them, Maxim and Sofeel, and Chilian's parents all dancing together.

She quickly fell into the rhythm of the familiar music, and together, as an almost perfectly working clock, the three pairs swayed around on the floor, in and out of formation, in spins and twirls, bows, and jumps, around the king and queen. Chilian led her as he had promised, and she couldn't help but love the way he looked as he danced. The way he was holding her by the waist and the way he would catch her as she fell from their jumps made her feel as if she could really fly.

Everything about that moment was perfect. She wanted to stay right there, by his side, dancing till her feet bled in the high heels. She wanted to feel him near, hear the music in her ears and be unbothered by the hundreds of eyes following her every move.

And as the dance slowed down a little, Chilian made sure that they were close enough for everyone to know that they weren't just friends. Because they weren't, and they both knew it.

She had read of this feeling a thousand times over. A feeling she was afraid of naming. Maybe she was naive. Maybe she jumped to conclusions about his feelings. But for someone who had never received even the slightest hint of approval and affection, this was more than anything she could have ever dreamt of.

This man would do anything for her, and she knew that now. And she realized that she would be there for him, for as long as he wanted her by his side. She would stay here with him in the palace, until the day he doesn't want her any more. Until the day where he gets tired of her. Because he deserved that kind of devotion. After everything he had given her. It was her turn to give.

And she would figure out what happened between them, all those years ago. She wanted to remember whatever happened, back then. Because every minute she had spent with him was priceless to her now. And if there were more of them buried deep inside her mind, she would find them all. She was determined. She would remember him.

*

Finally the music came to a stop.

The three couples also slowed their swaying and turned to face the king and queen. In a synchronized bow, they all paid their respects to the monarchs, and it was finally time for all the other nobles to join them. However, a quick and silent exchange between her and Chilian led to them quietly leaving the dancefloor. They decided to stand aside and enjoy the show, as drunk men and women, waltzed in between each other trying to make it look elegant.

It was the most fun she had all night.

The two of them talked and danced a little more throughout the night, discussing the recent events and her stay at the palace. They also told stories of times before their meeting, and Aimee sincerely enjoyed all the tales he had from the training grounds. Like how he and his friend Laurence had painted the instructors white horse red with paint, and how they were forced to wash it off themselves. He apparently gained a lot of respect for animals that day. He talked about all kinds of cuts and bruises he had gathered over the years and also about how King Aldrick himself sometimes had come down to spar with the three boys, Colyn, Chilian and Laurence.

She was fascinated by his life and by how fun it all sounded.

They were almost at the end of the dance and people had slowly started making their way to the dining hall, but many still remained in the festive ballroom.

"You want some?" Chilian asked as he handed her a glass of white wine.

"Yes, thank you. Although I'm not much of a drinker," she admitted.

"Really? I know a story of a certain someone who had to be walked home a few weeks ago," he said in a teasing tone.

"Are you mocking my drinking habits?"

"What? No, I would never mock a noblewoman. I'm a gentleman."

They laughed together as they sipped their expensive wine and looked out over the crowd.

In the midst of all the dancing figures emerged Sofeel, out of the elegant chaos. She looked a little tired and had trouble catching her breath. Her hair was also slowly coming apart, and Aimee could see how the sweat was shining off of her forehead.

She had never seen Sofeel in such a condition, as she had always been the pinnacle of elegance, but there was something awfully comforting about knowing that she too was a human, with imperfections.

She finally made her way to Aimee and Chilian, and in the time it took her, she regained some of her stability in breathing and stands.

Aimee did a little nod in her direction and Sofeel happily smiled at her. "About time," she said, directed at Chilian.

"What?" he asked in a nonchalant tone.

"I've been waiting for you to overthrow Maxim for all of my life, cousin, and you know it. Finally, I don't have to watch my every step." She turned towards Aimee, and a distinct smile appeared on her lips. "This is all because of you. Thank you, sister."

Aimee was taken aback by being called sister but laughed it off awkwardly. "I was only a minor part of the decision. Chilian would do what he found best for the kingdom, I just happened to get caught up in his business." She swayed her hand as to brush it off, but Sofeel didn't take it.

Without a warning she threw herself at both Chilian and Aimee and hugged them tightly. *"Thank you..."* she whispered to them. As she pulled away again, Aimee noticed her glazed eyes and her suspiciously red nose. She was on the verge of tears. "You will be a wonderful ruler, cousin," she said quietly.

Chilian looked down. "We both know you were born for the throne," he said. His words made the light in her eyes and the smile on her lips fade as the reality of her sad situation fell into place once again.

"If I was born for it, why was I born a woman?" she asked in a saddened voice.

"Who says women can't rule?" Aimee mumbled, not directed at anyone.

"The men."

Silence fell upon them.

The princess suddenly realized how she had ruined the mood, and quickly excused herself. She walked away slowly but spotted someone in the crowd. The noblewoman Aimee had seen Sofeel around quite a lot.

She finally recognized her as Claree Aestolas. She knew her as the daughter of a marquis working under her father back in Edenran. Their family had visited often so the men could talk about the work in the mountains.

She was the complete opposite of the princess, with dark brown skin and black curly hair. If Sofeel was a calm winter day, Claree would be a wild storm in the heat of the summer.

"They're lovers," Chilian whispered in her ears, as he had noticed Aimee's stare.

"What?" she asked in a little too loud of a voice.

Chilian nodded. "Three years they've been together. That's why Sofeel is dreading getting married to anyone, but her."

"Don't go around telling people that kind of thing! That's personal." Aimee warned, worried that anyone had heard them.

"Don't worry, it's common knowledge," Chilian said calmly.

"Still, would you go around telling people about my lover as if you were talking about the weather?" she asked, still a little angry at his random spilling of others' private information.

"Well, no, because that would mean you had a lover. And then I would have to scare him off, along with all your other suitors…"

Aimee turned around, her face boiling, only to see his smug smile being way too handsome to hate. She fisted her hand and gave him a hit in the side. He graciously pretended that it hurt a little and started giggling at her reaction.

"You're an ass, you know that?" she asked and turned around to face the crowd again.

"What a lousy mouth you have, should I silence it for you?"

he whispered next to her ear.

She wanted to pretend she didn't briefly consider it but stayed silent in her own shameless mind.

Without any warning, two arms wrapped around her shoulders in an embrace from behind. "Chilian what are you doing?" she asked, trying to shake him off. It would be too embarrassing if anyone saw them like that.

"Let go, someone will notice!" she whispered.

"Then let them," he whispered in a way too serious voice. He turned her around, so they now stood face to face, with his hands on her cheeks, to keep her from running away. "Let them know that we don't give a damn about them. Let them know that if they try and keep me away from you, they'll meet a quick end. Let them know that you're free to do whatever the hell you want."

His sudden speech completely swept her off the ground. She no longer felt her legs and it was like a swarm of butterflies was trying to make her fly away. Everything inside of her was screaming to stand up on her toes and lean the very last bit to close the distance between the two of them. She could feel his shaky breath on her nose. They were so close and yet those last centimeters felt as large as the seven seas.

Her heart was burning. His eyes burned even brighter. Aimee couldn't take it any more. She stood up on her toes.

But before she reached his lips she felt something grabbing her hair, and without any warning her head was yanked backwards, away from Chilian's warm hands and into a cold embrace she only knew too well.

A cold blade touched the skin of her throat as the warm blue eyes she had just looked into with burning desire, turned cold and hateful. She heard a few yells, and then the sound of a sword being drawn, as people around them gasped and screamed.

No.

*

He didn't know what to do. Suddenly, the blade had just found its way to his hand.

"What an affectionate display the two of you were putting on just now, am I right, doll?" Maxim whispered into Aimee's ear, as he was forcing her head further back. His eyes met Chilian.

"If you want your life spared you let go, right now…" Chilian mumbled, not able to hide the rage lurking under his skin. Aimee could barely see him, the way her head was held back by Maxim.

"You've never shown such a temper before, cousin," Maxim said with his disgusting smile. Chilian was going to cut it off.

Aimee rightfully looked terrified. Everyone around them looked frightened as the three of them slowly circled each other. Chilian had always been the better fighter, but would he be able to hit Maxim, without him using Aimee as a shield?

The music had died, and everyone was dead silent as they waited for Chilian to engage. The only real noise was the sound of Aimee's frantic breathing and vivid attempts of keeping up as she was almost dragged across the floor by Maxim.

With the knife to her throat, she had no chance of using any of the skills Chilian had taught her.

He cursed himself for not considering that possibility.

"I will make you bleed…" he whispered through his teeth, as he watched Maxim gently stroking the neck of the woman he loved.

"Then I'll make her bleed first," he smiled as he moved the

knife up along her skin and pressed it against her jaw. Chilian felt everything inside of him screaming, wanting, longing, to see Maxim dead on the ground.

Guards had surrounded them, and he could see Sofeel and Claree looking terrified in the crowd behind them. His father was there, tense as the situation slowly escalated.

"*Chili...*" Aimee whispered, trying to hold back the tears that were filling her eyes. The guards were confused as to who they should help. Chilian knew all of them personally as he had trained with them the last decade, but they were still loyal to the crown. And as far as they knew, Maxim was the crown prince of Oplia.

Maxim's laugh rung throughout the ballroom, cold and demonic. "How would you feel if I did this?" Maxim asked as he slowly added the pressure on the knife he was holding against Aimee's chin.

"YOU LET GO OF HER!" Chilian screamed, overtaken by the rage burning up his flesh and bones.

But Maxim kept pressing, until small drops of blood started running down Aimee's neck.

That was the last straw. Chilian ran towards them both, not caring what would happen next, only focusing on Maxim's throat, which in a few seconds would leave his head rolling around on the ground, with that smug smile wiped off completely.

He swung his sword. It all happened slowly. Maxim stepped to the right with Aimee, avoiding Chilian's blade. Behind his cousin, two blue eyes appeared out of nowhere. White hair floating through the air.

Chilian heard a yell. Then another. Maxim was laughing behind him.

Silence.

The king's expression changed. He collapsed onto the floor. A loud thud rung throughout the silent hall. A red pool slowly seeping out from under him. Then the screams began. First by Queen Alryn who had been running up behind the king until then. Then Sofeel's cries rung out as she ran towards her injured father. Then as people started to realize what had happened, they all started yelling and screaming for help, from some sort of medical personnel.

Chilian clenched onto his sword, still dripping a dreadful red. Everyone started moving around. He couldn't see the king any more, as his body was now covered by a swarm of people. He couldn't see if he was alive or not. Chilian's blade had slashed him, but Chilian wasn't sure where. *The chest? The throat maybe?*

He heard someone being dropped next to him. Aimee was laying on the floor. She looked terrified. He thought he wanted to help her up, but he couldn't move an inch. His gaze rose up to see the devil's pale lips taunting him. He had known this would happen. He had planned it all. He tricked him.

His rage rung louder in his ears, than the cries of his aunt and cousin behind him. His grip tightened around the blade's handle. Aimee seemed to understand his intention, but she didn't try to stop him. Good.

But he didn't get to take a single step before something hard hit him in the back of the head. For a moment it was like the entire world was both falling and fading away from him at the same time. Aimee's scream and frightened look was obscured into a black void and everything went dark.

The last he remembered was the sound of agony.

Chapter 15

Two Kinds of Prison

His body hit the floor almost like a boulder. She couldn't help but let out a loud sound reminiscent of a scream or a whine.

The guard who had knocked him out with his sword, looked as stunned as everyone around them. Other guards came running in to assist him, and Aimee realized that they were gonna drag Chilian away from her. Down into a dark and dirty cell to rot. She tried crawling towards him, tried to hold him down and out of the guard's reach, but her trembling body didn't allow it.

The scene had burned itself onto her mind. The royal women crying over the king's dying body. The many doctors and medics trying their best to save him. The guards looking confused and terrified. And lastly her Chilian laying deadly still on the floor in front of her.

She started crawling. One hand, one leg. Towards the only man that mattered.

But a white boot came crashing down on her left hand. She felt the bones shattering inside of it, on impact. This time she let out a proper scream, loud enough to turn a few heads. But not enough to overdo the other people's cries around her.

Maxim's face came into view in front of her. His boot came crashing down once again, sending agony through her entire body. Maybe it was the pain corrupting her mind. but his smile didn't look human any more. It was sick and twisted, his eyes looking insane with hatred and madness. The cold eyes told her everything she needed to know. This was over. Her freedom, gone once again. And this time, he had no limits. No restriction. Aldrick had never made the official announcement. Nobody knew the heritage had changed.

Maxim Istatis would be king.

And she was now completely at his mercy.

He said something. She didn't hear it. The pain and fear and shock rung louder in her ears, than any tyrants' words. Five men came over, picked up the king and carried him away from the accident scene. She looked back to realize that the guards were about to drag away Chilian's equally lifeless body. She felt her lips move in protest, but nothing came out. She was weak. She was helpless, there on the floor. All she was strong enough to do was keeping back her tears. And cradle the broken hand as tightly as she could to numb the unbearable pain. Before she realized it, Chilian was gone.

She was alone.

Finally, some hands picked her up too and dragged her away from the chaos. She didn't remember any of the walk up to her room. Only that the hands placed her down on the floor in her prison, and the sound of the doors locking behind her. She saw her maids come running like a group of obscure shadows, dancing around the room, in weird blurry movements. She remembered standing up with a lot of help. Getting undressed, and her hair being brushed. The makeup was wiped from her face, and a woman in white, wrapped three metal pins, the size of knitting needles, around her hand with bandages.

She was given some liquid, probably a kind of medicine, and then she was left lying on the bed. It was like the silence slowly crept in through her skin and flesh, quietly making her go mad.

The sounds of the screams and chaos in the ballroom haunted her there in the stillness. The sight of both the king and Chilian lying on the floor, was probably gonna be with her til the day she died. She couldn't make out if her mind was completely quiet, not wanting to process it, or if all of the thoughts were simply too fast and loud to even hear.

But one thought ran through her, clear as the blade Chilian had swung, just a few minutes before.

Where was he now?

Had he been killed? Was he locked up somewhere, still unconscious? Was he cold, and in the dark, scared to death? Or was he being doomed to be hanged in a square somewhere in the streets of Tessas? Would she see him again, in one piece, or would their next encounter be at his own funeral? Or hers maybe?

That made another thought come to mind. *What would Maxim do to her now?* The expression he made after the incident was clearly one of pure madness. And how he without any hesitation had shattered her hand showed her his true violent nature. He had been holding back previously. Everything up till now was just a taste of his temper. She was going to die in this palace. Within these walls. There was no doubt.

Suddenly, without warning, tears started blurring her vision again. Small sobs made their way up her throat, and before she could gain the strength to hold them back, they turned to loud cries of pain and misery.

She wanted to return home. Grab Chilian's hand and run as fast as possible. Back to her flower fields and her little pond in the corner of the garden.

She should have followed him that day. Through the door in the wall. Away from this place.

When she left Leirath to go to Tessas, she thought she would have a good time at a masquerade, be happy away from her family, and finally find her place in the world. But because she was dumb enough to take a stroll late at night, the king was probably dead now, and a tyrant was going to run the kingdom to the ground. This was all her fault. So many people would suffer under Maxim's rule, and she was the one to blame.

Children would be orphaned, towns wiped away with hunger and disease, and parents forced to sacrifice themselves for their kids' survival. Both the economy and infrastructure would be ruined, and everyone would live in pain and poverty.

As the scope of what she had done, and how much blood there would be on her hands, came to light, everything started crashing down around her.

The ceiling, the walls, and the furniture, crumbled and fell as she crept in under the covers. She didn't want to be there any more. Didn't want to be the reason for any of this.

She wished she had never existed.

She closed her eyes and let herself drift away to a better place. A place where she would never hurt anyone again.

The floor was cold.

It smelled like a mix of wet hay and puke, and the darkness didn't help the atmosphere at all. He slowly tried to stand up, but he felt a sharp pain in the back of his head, forcing him back onto the ground.

Everything was a big fuss. Nothing felt normal, and he didn't know what was going on.

He reached down to take a hold of his sword but discovered it to be gone. So was the knife that usually rested in his boot.

As his eyes slowly got used to the darkness, he could make out certain things around him. Like the cold, gray stones making out the walls around him. The stack of hay in one corner and the iron bars blocking his way to freedom. The dungeon.

At first he was confused as to his new surroundings. But then it slowly started coming back to him. About Maxim. How Chilian was about to cut off his head, and how he slashed the king instead.

His uncle had probably heard the yells and the blades being drawn from across the dancefloor and had rushed over to break up the fight. For that he would probably never open his eyes again.

So what now? King Aldrick was supposed to announce Chilian's claim as the new heir. The rest of the royal family knew it, but Maxim would probably have them punished with treason for trying to convince others. The entire court probably still believed Maxim was the rightful heir. And Chilian… the king's murderer.

The thought hit him twice as hard as the thing that knocked him out. He would be convicted in court with Maxim as the judge. He would be hanged or maybe decapitated for an accident.

But there had been so many people around to witness it. They saw what happened, they knew the truth. Would they be able to save him from Maxim's scheme?

Or should he say King Maxim? The title felt like poison on his tongue. He had always known he would have to call him that someday, but now, he felt disgusted. That bastard basically killed his own father through Chilian's blade. He knew exactly what was going to happen as soon as he pulled Aimee away from him. He had planned all of this…

Wait. *Aimee.*

His blood ran cold.

His hand shot to his collar, searching for the small pin. After a little fumbling, his fingers found the pearl's white surface, and he took it off to look at it. It didn't shine in the dark cell, as it did in the sun, but it was still nice and smooth as always. Traces of Aimee's red lipstick still clung onto the smooth surface. She had been right there in his arms. *How did he lose her so quickly? Why did he just let go when Maxim came and took her for himself?*

In his mind, Chilian saw the reflection of the blade, Maxim was holding to her chin. It had cut through her delicate skin, drawing blood, redder than her hair, and it had probably hurt like hell.

He remembered her shining eyes, on the verge of tears as the last thing before everything went black. How didn't he see all of this coming? How didn't he stop the blade before impact with King Aldrick?

He had a little hope that the king had survived. He had survived three years in war and led a force against the rebellion, Chilian was forced to flee from ten years ago. He had been through hell on earth, so a single slash to the chest in a freak accident shouldn't be any more significant than a small paper cut.

But he was old and sickly. Everyone knew. And everyone knew he wasn't the brave, undefeatable knight he once was.

Quick footsteps rung throughout the long corridor on the other side of the iron bars. A warm light and the sound of a torch came with them and finally a cloaked figure appeared before him. The light burned his eyes and it was only when the figure spoke, he knew.

"What the hell happened? I'm on patrol for two hours and you kill Alrick?"

"Nice to see you too, Laurence…" Chilian mumbled.

"I know I'm usually the jokester here, but this isn't the time, and you know it!" Laurence whispered in an angry manner.

"Listen, the Keepers down here are ruthless, so I only have a few minutes before they come and drag me out by the ankles."

He was right about the dungeon guards known as the Keepers. Due to their hostile behavior to prisoners and their pale skin, many feared them. Most people blamed the lack of sunlight, others just called them crazy.

Maybe Maxim could find some friends down here…

"Okay, Laurence, listen to me," he mumbled, a lot more serious this time. "I need to know three things. First of all, how long has it been?" Laurence had to think for a second, 'cause he probably wasn't sure of the exact time.

"I would say it's been about three hours," Laurence finally answered.

Chilian nodded. "And the king?" he asked, terrified of the answer.

"They say he is still alive but struggling. The blade apparently struck down the end of his neck, and further along his chest." Chilian took a deep breath. As long as he wasn't dead yet, the king could still make the announcement. Dethrone his tyrant son and make sure his beloved kingdom wasn't cast into chaos.

"What's the last question?" Laurence asked, effectively pulling him out of his train of thought.

He took a breath. "Aimee? Do you know anything about her? Her whereabouts?"

He didn't like how long it took Laurence to answer.

"I think some people heard her scream and saw her getting dragged off by some guards. That's all I've heard since I *just* got back from my shift."

His hands tightened around the iron bars. "Can you do me a favor?" Chilian asked.

"Of course."

"Keep me updated. On everything. And try to keep her safe? The best you can."

Laurence sighed. "I don't think you understand how serious this situation is yet. I can't promise anything."

Chilian unconsciously held his breath. She was all alone.

Laurence stared at him in the light of the torch. "I don't think you've ever cared so much for anyone."

Chilian smiled by the thought of it. Laurance was right that his infatuation with her was almost like a curse, but he was okay with it. "Just promise me."

"All right. As long as you promise to get out of this mess, with your head still attached."

Silence rung throughout the corridor.

"Of course…"

They both recognized the hesitation in his voice, but no one dared to mention it.

"I'll see you tomorrow, old friend."

He stood up and walked away. When Laurence turned to look back at him, Chilian could have sworn he saw tears slowly forming in the corner of his eyes.

A quick nod of acknowledgement sent him on his way, and Chilian was left in the dark with his own thoughts screaming louder than the rats cluttering the floor.

This was probably his last night before hell would swallow him up in court. So he lied down on the dirty floor and tried to enjoy the silence before the storm.

*

"So it's been five hours? And the doctors only just announced it?"

"Apparently, the prince kept them from telling everyone. I don't know why, though."

Aimee recognized Linari and Lilly's familiar voices as she slowly opened her eyes.

"You mean the king?" Sheldy sharply corrected Lilly.

"Wait, has he already gained that title?" Linari asked in a scared tone.

"The moment his late Majesty died he became king, yes," Sheldy explained.

"How horrible…" Lilly mumbled loud enough to put the room to silence. "I'm scared for Aimee. What do you think he'll do to her?" she continued.

She quietly opened her eyes to see Linari hug Lilly, and whisper something in her ear.

Sheldy sighed. "With no restrictions left, he is sure to go wild. I can only imagine our lady being the punching bag for him from now on. If we're lucky he'll leave us alone."

"How can you say that?" Lilly asked in disgust.

"Hey. I just don't want my family involved in this. This is her business."

Aimee had had enough. "Linari, Sheldy, leave please."

The three maids jumped, when they realized that she had heard everything they said.

Linari and Sheldy quickly excused themselves, leaving Lilly alone in the room with her.

She remembered the day she came in with her old nanny to serve her breakfast. Aimee was finally old enough to not need her nanny any more, so Lilly had begun as her personal maid instead. She had been very hesitant in the start but over the years she had been working for the Achilleas, she had opened up a ton to reveal a bubbly and loyal personality.

She had been a great support in this time, helping her with establishing a daily routine, and instructing the other maids in how to best care for her. Aimee should probably give her a raise when they got out of there.

If they got out…

"How is your hand today, Aimee?" she asked, snapping her out of her terrifying thoughts.

"It hurts…" Aimee said exhausted and tried to close the aching hand. She looked out of the window as Lilly gently started massaging her arm and wrist. It was completely dark outside, the only light illuminating the trees beneath, being the moon hanging over The Palace Of Dreams.

Her room was also sparsely lit, with only a few candles here and there, but other than that it was dark, and unwelcoming.

"The doctor says it's only a fracture, but it'll hurt for at least another five weeks. I'm very sorry." Lilly said next to her.

"You shouldn't be sorry… You should be angry. Furious," Aimee said without looking away from the window.

"At his Majesty?" Lilly asked in a timid voice.

Aimee nodded. "Just don't go around showing it…" she whispered.

"All right, Aimee."

A bit of silence went on as the women had run out of words to exchange. Aimee felt awkward so she had to fill the empty void with something useful.

"So the king is dead?" she asked bluntly.

"…Yes, sadly…"

Aimee tried clenching her fractured hand to feel another pain, than the one inside of her chest, as the reality sunk in. The last week she had been getting a little *too* used to world shattering revelations, but this probably outweighed most of them.

A chilling thought went through her mind, and the warm body covered in blankets started trembling.

"What happened to Chilian...?" she whispered, as Lilly's answer would mean life or death for her.

"No one has heard from Sir Malvaria since the incident. Although rumors have gone amongst the other servants, that he is being kept in the dungeons, and watched carefully by the Keepers."

Aimee felt her worries fade a little, as she realized that nothing serious would happen to him before a proper trial would be conducted. Which luckily could take days to prepare, if not weeks.

A sigh of relief left her lips. Although she wanted to see his cheeky smile before her, the knowledge of him being safe for now was a big relief. She tried to think of something she could hold close to her until then. Maybe something he had touched?

She remembered back to the day in the flower field where they had relaxed together in the baking sun. He had pulled out a little purple box with a pair of earrings.

Aimee had worn them here and there, but she didn't want to risk damaging them, or potentially losing them, so they had taken a prominent place on her makeup table, where she could admire them when getting ready for the day.

"Lilly, could you fetch me the box over there," she requested, pointing with her healthy hand towards the table with the giant mirror.

"Of course." As she rushed over on her little quest, Aimee struggled a bit before sitting up with her new disability. As Lilly turned around again, she made a terrified expression and rushed back over. "Aimee, you mustn't sit up, the doctor specifically told us to have you rest!" she said frantically, while trying to figure out the safest way to get her back in a lying position.

"I'm still resting. Now I'm just a little more mobile," she said laughing to herself over the irony in that sentence.

Lilly handed over the purple box, and Aimee opened it to find the two pink gemstones shining up at her. The silver-threads forming the circular patterns looked golden in the dim candle light. The clear crystals between the pink gems and the hooks, still puzzled her mind. *Was it actually diamonds?*

With a lot of struggling, she almost succeeded in getting one of them to hang on to her ear, but Lilly wouldn't have it, and took over.

"Honestly, this isn't the time for jewelry," she said, almost annoyed.

A sigh of relief left Aimee as she could feel Chilian being a little closer than before. Not a whole great closer, but just enough to calm her.

But Lilly looked tense. And that was understandable.

"I want to talk to you," Aimee began, after gaining the courage she needed.

Lilly gulped as she sat down on a nearby stool, as she did when they occasionally chatted at her father's estate. This time, however, it was more than gossip from the kitchen and talks of interests.

She sighed. "Now that *he...* is king. Things here will change. I and anyone associated with me will be in constant fear of the unknown," she explained, "I'm giving you this chance now. If you want to go home and see your family. Find a new job and start fresh without any intervention from me and my problems, you can. I will try and arrange a carriage to take you back, as soon as possible. You have been a loyal servant to me and the closest thing I've ever had to a friend, so you deserve a chance at life beyond this prison. I'll give you a day to consider it, okay?" she said while studying Lilly's facial expressions.

Her round face looked both disgusted and allured by the offer, all at once, and Aimee knew she had placed a difficult choice on her shoulders.

"Thank you, Aimee," she said, while facing the floor.

Aimee managed a faint smile. "Any other things I should be aware of this evening?"

"This night, actually," Lilly corrected, "It's around midnight now. The doctors announced the king dead about half an hour ago, and our new ruler hasn't been seen since."

"He is probably preparing for his take-over…"

"Miss, I wasn't there. I've heard a lot of rumors, but I don't know anything concrete other than that."

Aimee nodded. "Of course." She let out a loud sigh. "You're free to go, I'll call if I need any assistance. Please return with an answer, as soon as possible."

Lilly hesitated to leave her injured employer all alone, but she probably wanted some rest too, after the day of preparations for the catastrophic ball. So she did a quick nod and sprinted out through the door.

She looked back over her shoulder one last time before she disappeared out into the chaos that was the outside.

And left Aimee alone to her thoughts.

She felt the earrings weighing down on her ears as her vision blurred. Not by tears, not by rage, but by pure numbness. She should scream, cry, and curse, break every expensive thing within reach and try to reach down to the dungeons to see Chilian again. But instead she sat completely still, staring out into the dim nothingness.

It was like she was gone. Out of her own body and on a

different level. Like she was above it all. Like none of this was even her business.

Everything was just cloudy as she felt nothing. As she removed herself from the reality she was trapped in. It was awfully comforting to her.

But for some reason her head wouldn't allow her to stay in that safe place for long. Because just as fast as she had faded away, she appeared again, back in her own body and her thoughts started hammering on her mind.

Thoughts of the future, and the present, the people around her and herself.

It hurt. Everything hurt. She was hungry. She was beat up. And she felt more miserable than ever before.

She took off the blanket and swung her legs out over the bedside. With wary steps she walked over to the mirror and sat down at the table.

She looked absolutely horrible. With her messy hair, bangs under her eyes and a bandage covering the wound, left by Maxim's knife during the chaos. She was a complete mess.

She couldn't even cry about her looks, as most other noble women would have done in her situation. The most emotion she managed to show was her face frowning at her own pettiness, before laying her head down on the table and closing her eyes. This was all a nightmare, she convinced herself. She just needed to rest for a little bit, and when she woke up again, she would return to her normal, meaningless life in Leirath.

She couldn't wait.

The warm sun burned her eyes.

Elniba and her father looked unfaced by it. They were both high and mighty as they stood and awaited the carriage to make its way through the front doors.

It was small and black, driven by a brown horse, and packed with about four luggage bags. They weren't very well attached, hinting at the fact that they had been packed in a hurry.

Finally the driver, a little robust man, stopped the vehicle in front of the three of them. She could hear the group of maids whispering behind them, as he stepped down to open the door for the people inside.

A pretty woman with long, blond, almost white hair stepped out onto the gravel, wearing a simple gray dress. Her father, Erlan, stepped toward her, handing her a hand as she struggled getting a proper balance in her high heels.

"Welcome to Leirath, Lady Difis. It's an honor to have you," he said calmly as she finally stood firm.

"Thank you so much and sorry for the short notice. The situation escalated far faster than we had expected, and we really had no other place to go."

"Of course. I'm just happy you made it out alive. Where is your husband?" her father asked the lady.

"He stayed behind with Aldrick to fight them off. He didn't want to be a coward and leave his friend behind," she said with a saddened expression.

"Of course, if I didn't agree to take care of the two of you, I would join them in a heartbeat," he said in a passionate voice. Aimee never heard him talking like that, other than when talking about Mother. Aimee wished he would talk about her mother more.

"Lady Difis, I would like you to meet my girls." Aimee heard him say, and she looked up. He walked over behind them and placed a hand on their shoulders. " This is my eldest, Elniba, and Aimee, my youngest. I hope they will keep the young lord

entertained during your stay."

He nodded to someone, and she finally noticed the boy, standing in the door of the carriage. He had been too quiet for her to notice earlier.

He had dark brown hair and pretty blue eyes, matching his mother's. A relatively new wound went down his left eye, and he looked pale and tired, probably after the long journey in the small carriage.

"Come here, darling," the woman said softly, "we'll be staying with these kind people for a while, so you should say thank you."

The boy looked a little timid, but quickly bowed his head, and mumbled some kind of thanks.

"Chilian, be louder. Nobody likes someone who mumbles, you know that," the lady said, but he remained quiet.

Aimee looked at the boy a little older than herself. Elniba, to her side, looked uninterested and the rising silence rang louder and louder. He clearly felt uncomfortable in the situation, and she didn't want him to have that kind of first impression.

She stepped forward and walked up to him with a big smile. "Hello, I'm Aimee. Would you like me to show you your room?" she asked and reached out her hand, "I walked past it earlier, and it's really nice. I promise."

The people around her remained quiet and the boy looked at her with a certain shyness. Or wariness.

She couldn't tell.

Finally, his pretty blue eyes lit up, and he gently took her hand.

A smile matching her own appeared upon his lips and she let him away, and towards the big doors. On the way she caught a glimpse of her father. A face of approval. Her heart's flame grew by the simple expression.

Elniba still looked unfaced by everything and clearly wasn't interested in anything having to do with the boy. Good, Aimee thought to herself. Then she would have him all to herself.

She looked back over her shoulder. The boy still looked shy, and tired, but there was definitely a lively spirit in him. A fun one.

She was so excited to finally have a friend.

Chapter 16

Men in Shadows

The warm sun tickled her skin.

The sharp rays of light burned her eyes as she slowly opened them again. What time was it? How long had she been asleep for?

She took a hand to her confused head and tried making sense of it all.

"What a peculiar place to sleep."

She jumped out of her seat at the table, tossing over the chair she had sat on and tumbling hard to the cold floor. Without thinking, she tried to catch herself with her injured hand, and she once again felt the incredible pain of her bones shaking and shattering all throughout it.

"Well I must say, never have a lady *actually* fallen for me. How funny."

She was lost for words as the new king of Oplia stood and stared down at her in the doorframe. He looked awfully tired, and his usually straight and perfect hair was messy and all over the place. She guessed taking over a kingdom in a single night was a lot more work than what he was used to.

"Your Majesty, I didn't expect you here so soon…" she mumbled, trying to regain her composure.

"Oh, did you really think I would forget about my favorite toy just because of a small incident? I would neverOh yeah, about yesterday." He moved closer, and she tried backing away into a corner. "I'm sorry, my dear," he continued, "you were supposed to be yesterday's star, opening the dance with me, and sitting by my side at the dinner afterwards, but after my cousin's little stunt, throwing me off the pole, I had to prioritize. I hope you'll forgive me…" he said as he leaned down in front of her and gently stroked her cheek.

She wanted to bite his fingers off.

"Of course…" she said, scared of what he'd do if she didn't respond.

His eyes suddenly gained some kind of remorse, as he gently ran a finger over the wound he had given her. "I do apologize for my treatment of you yesterday. I really just needed a reaction from Chilian."

She couldn't help herself but ask, "What happened to him?"

His smile widened by her question. "Well we couldn't just let a king's murderer run around freely. So I locked him up, somewhere dark, where he will await his trial," he explained relaxed.

She felt her fists clenching against the ground hurting her immensely. "Trial? When?" she asked with maybe too much spite in her voice.

"Sometime in the coming days. I'll be the judge of course."

Her heart stopped.

"You…" She couldn't even continue the sentence as she already knew what this meant for Chilian. Certain death. He would never let him live. Not ever.

His smile was too wide for his own good. It was haunting. Like it had gone off the rails but still sane. Such a disturbing combination.

He was close now. Too close for comfort. Not that she was ever comfortable with him being within ten miles of her.

He opened his mouth. "You know… A king needs a queen." She froze. Completely.

"I don't want that…" she whispered without thinking. He simply let out a small chuckle.

"I'm afraid there's no other path for you, doll." Then he leaned closer. Grabbed the back of her neck, holding her still. She didn't do anything. Didn't resist, didn't push him away. She wasn't there. She didn't want to be there.

She disappeared from her body again.

His cold lips touched hers. Finally a single tear fell from her eye. Once again a warm liquid emerged from her lip, as he bit down upon her lip, reopening the wound. The red blood dripped down, coloring her neck, and nightgown.

She just watched from above. Feeling empty.

He slowly pulled back, away from her, licking the red off his lips.

"You taste delicious, doll" he said nonchalantly.

"I hate you," she whispered again, without thinking of the consequences.

His smile turned soft for a moment. Tender almost. "I know. Who could ever love a monster, right?" he laughed. "But you'll learn to endure me. Or you'll fade and die like a leaf in autumn," he said while tightening the grip around her neck.

He once again forced himself upon her, in a quick kiss on the cheek and walked away. "A king has many duties, I'm afraid. So I'll have to visit you again another time. Actually, I came to give you this." He reached down into his pocket where he pulled out a brown bun. "Since you didn't get to eat at the banquet, you could probably use something to keep you alive. Who knows, if you behave, maybe I'll nullify my punishment. You do look a little thin…"

She didn't respond.

He tossed her the bun and walked towards the door with heavy steps. "See you later, my doll," he said in an upbeat tone.

She didn't respond.

And just like that, she was left alone again.

The bun he had tossed her smelled delicious, and she didn't know if she could leave it like last time. The hunger was slowly consuming her, and every second she stared at it the larger the urge grew. Finally, she gave in and took a bite of the newly baked bun. She didn't care that she gave Maxim another victory. Survival was more important than pride.

The white interior of the bread was colored red, as the blood kept dripping.

She sat there in the corner eating, completely engulfed in her own thoughts, which were loud enough for the maid's door to swing open without her noticing. Neither did she notice the dark shadow slowly creeping up behind her.

It was only when she felt a tap on her shoulder, that she turned around, in a heartbeat, screaming at the top of her lungs, at the intruder. However, he was quick and held a hand to her mouth to keep her quiet.

How could she let not only one but two men sneak up on her, without even the feeling of goosebumps warning her?

She tried to struggle out of the man's grasp, hurting her hand further in the process, and called for help from the guards outside her door. But his grip around her mouth was too tight for any sound to escape. He tried to calm her down. "I am not here to hurt you, miss," he said. Suddenly, he pulled down his black hood to reveal a handsome and tanned face, staring at her, concerned.

She recognized the Dahlian family's characteristic amber

eyes and realized who he was immediately afterwards.

"Chilian send me. I'm a friend."

He gently removed his hand allowing her to both scream and shout, but she didn't.

"Laurence Dahlian? You're friends with Chilian?" she asked, still shaken over his sudden appearance.

He nodded with a smile. "Practically grew up with the guy. And let me tell you, never before has he been more obsessed with anyone in his life. You're almost all he ever talks about. It's quite annoying actually." He laughed and sat down beside her. "Also what happened to your lip?"

Aimee didn't answer.

He recognized her silence and simply handed her a handkerchief to clean up the blood.

She was still wary of the situation but decided to go with it. "You said he sent you? Is he all right?" she asked, thirsty for details of the outside world.

"Right now, yes. He is managing. But he is locked in one of the cells in the underground dungeons. I only got by the guards on the promise of a hefty bribe. Where I'll find the money, I have no idea of."

She sighed in relief. "So he isn't hurt?"

"No, only that blow to the head he received. He'll be fine if he makes it past the trial." He rested up against the wall next to her, as if they were old friends having a heart to heart.

"Do you know when it's gonna be held?" she asked.

"Sometime next week, if we're lucky. Probably before Aldrick's funeral," he answered.

She hesitated.

" You and Chilian talk so casually about him. Was he a good man?" Aimee had never met the king before last night. They only spoke briefly and now he was gone. He had seemed kind and caring, and Chilian seemed to have had a great load of respect for him. So he must've been good.

"Extraordinary. He treated me, Chili, and Colyn as his own sons. He would come down to train with us when he had time, and when Chilian was old enough, he let him be part of his council meetings. Eventually, he gave Chilian a position as one of his councilmen. Probably in the hopes he would change his mind about the throne. A big day for the guy, let me tell you. He also knighted both of us. Only the finest to do the job, am I right?" He laughed and puffed Aimee in the side. He was so casual about it and made Chilian look like a stiff gentleman.

He spoke with both wits and passion, and it was clear to her that he admired the both of them a great deal.

"You're going to miss him, aren't you?" she asked, trying to reach a deeper level with him.

He hesitated for a moment before answering, "He was like a Father when my real one wasn't around..."

She nodded.

Laurence quickly cleared his throat, embarrassed by the emotions he had let come to the surface. "Now what I was supposed to do here was actually check on you. Has the bastard done anything? I heard him leave just before." He paused for a moment. "He obviously did that, didn't he?" he said pointing to her lip. The blood had finally stopped under the pressure of the hankerchief.

"Yeah, I had fallen asleep, and he was just suddenly there," she said as she waved her hand around, "he has an ugly habit of appearing out of nowhere."

Laurence laughed. "He has always been like that. A little creep."

A slight giggle escaped her. "Well, he cut open my cheek, bit my lip, twice, and put me through hell on earth. Oh, and he fractured my hand, apparently." She raised her left hand, as to show the very distasteful joke she was laughing at. Laurence just looked concerned though.

"Chilian isn't gonna take that lightly…" he mumbled, and sat back up against the wall.

"Why not?" she asked.

"Because I think he would throw himself as a stepping stone, if it meant your shoes wouldn't be dirtied."

"Really?"

"Absolutely."

They both giggled.

A moment's reflection later, and they both sat with heavy shoulders under the situation's enormous pressure. "I should get going before anyone notices me. I'm a very recognizable face around here," he said and stood up.

"Why?"

"Let's just say that I'm a charmer," he said with a cheesy smile, "I hope I charmed you too, miss."

"Sure, we can say that."

His smile turned tender, and he made his way towards the small door.

"I'll be keeping an eye out for you and try to relay information and love letters between you two. I better get paid after all of this." he said with a smug face.

A thought popped into her head as he finished the sentence. She stood up and told Laurence to stay where he was, and not move an inch. She left him in confusion and made her way to the office on the other side of the entrance hall.

The furniture was still moved to the sides for their makeshift training area.

She quickly picked up a pen and scribbled out a short letter. She then sealed it and rushed back to Laurence impatiently laying on her bed waiting.

She handed him the paper and said, "Please, make sure this reaches him. It's all I know so far, and some things I need to tell him before it may be too late, to do in person."

He hesitantly took it and stared at it for a while. He looked back up at her with a sincere face which spoke volumes.

"You are truly something, aren't you?" he said with an impressed voice, "if you mean as much to Chilian as he says, I'll make sure to honor you with the respect worthy of a queen," he said. He took her good hand and placed a quick and formal kiss on the back of her hand. And without another word he disappeared down the dark tunnel, only lit by what looked like candle light.

She felt a sense of relief wash over her, as she realized that she had gained another ally in the snake's cold prison. And now that she had a connection to Chilian through this new ally, she could finally breathe somewhat calmly.

But calm was never long in this place, because her doors suddenly flew open and revealed her five maids rushing in, Lilly leading them all, and shouting.

"WE KNOW THE DATE!"

*

Chilian, I am relieved to know that you aren't hurt, and that you are still breathing.

Laurence has just told me of your whereabouts, and though it calms me to know, it does not change the fact that there is nothing I can do for you. I can't raise an army, or bribe a guard to secure your escape, as I myself am a prisoner once again.

I'm afraid your work and sacrifices were all in vain, and that I've cost you nothing, but pain and danger.

I hold your earrings close to me at this moment, as it is the only thing I have left of you to carry with me. You have never shown me anything but kindness and affection, and in a painful life of rejection, and favoritism, this has meant more to me than anything else in life.

I hope to see you again to thank you in person. But I fear that our next meeting will be in an unfair court, with a corrupted ruler to pass our judgment.

Do not worry for me in this hour, but focus on your own health and wellbeing. I hope that we will be able to meet again, under much better circumstances. But for now, I will send you my love with these words. Stay strong for me, and return as you always have done.

Yours truly.
Aimee.

Chilian read through it again for the tenth time, making sure he didn't miss a single comma, or pencil stroke. He could see, where tears had blurred the ink, and how her frantic hand had smeared out some of the words.

He too had felt tears, when he first read the letter in what felt like days ago. Laurence hadn't returned since he had been there with it, and had told him of Aimee's fragile condition. And of course the news of the king's passing. His trial was to start in about three days, but with no apparent sunlight, in the dark cell, telling the days apart had proven almost impossible.

The food he was served was also something out of a beggar's

cup, consisting of disturbing soup, and bread harder than the stones around him.

He had had worse, yes, but it was still almost enough for him to admit his sins, and get the execution over with.

But he kept telling himself that he had to stay alive. Not just for Aimee, but also for everyone else too. Right now he was probably the only one with enough followers and supporters to have an actual claim to the throne Maxim sat upon. If he didn't get out of this mess, everyone would suffer. All of the people in Oplia would be guaranteed an even harder life than what they already had, and it would no doubt lead to unpleasant fights and demonstrations in the streets, followed by famine, death and illness.

He had been out among the common people a few times before. On patrols and undercover as a butcher's boy. And every single time had he heard about the worries of the people. They all feared Maxim's rule and saw him as an incompetent party animal that would run the country into the ground. Although he was more of a tyrant than those poor people could ever prepare for.

He had to save them, somehow. Them and Aimee. His Blossom. His people.

He leaned his back up against the cold, moist wall, and looked out into the darkness. He missed his silky sheets in his warm bed next to the beautiful fireplace. His clean clothes and bathtub in the bathroom were also on his mind, as he seemed to get dirtier, every single time he even moved. He imagined Aimee, waiting for him as he stepped through the doors of his chambers, ready to embrace him, and talk all night long about all of her thoughts and dreams. He would hold her tight and listen as her voice would be like a lullaby in his ears.

His daydream shifted locations to his childhood home, the small town of Chission, where Aimee was lying in the grass behind a small mansion, sunbathing in the south's warmth.

A quiet place, away from the palace and her father. Away from his parents too, and with no one to rule over them. He would be Archduke of Stillgate, and he would have the means to take proper care of her. He would let her do whatever she wanted and would support her in all of her decisions and ideas.

That was the future he wanted. The future she deserved. But as it looked now, that future was drifting further and further away by the minute.

If he were not executed by next month, he would be imprisoned in that palace for the rest of his life, and Aimee would have no one to help her. Maxim would rule and everything would crumble under him.

And if Chilian somehow reclaimed the throne, he would be stuck in a position he didn't want. He would be able to send Aimee away if she wanted it, but if she didn't, they would both be stuck inside the stone walls.

The future looked grim, and that was all he could figure out at that point. He went on thinking about it, for what felt like another week, until the keepers finally came to unlock his cage. They led him up to the bright surface, where he would breathe his last few breaths before the trial.

*

The dress sat uncomfortably tight around her torso as they made their way down the long hall. It was a black affair, with long heavy fabric, and little to no gems to shine off of it. Everything except her neck and head were covered, and her long sleeves hung loose around her arms most likely to cover the bandages around her hand.

The only jewelry she had been allowed to wear was a single pair of earrings. So, of course she had chosen the pink ones. Both in a silent protest to what were about to happen, but also to have Chilian close in these last moments, before all hell broke loose.

Maxim was wearing a black suit, with a long coat, and white ruffles in the front. A sapphire moon-like brooch was displayed around his neck, and he was carrying his decorated sword to his side.

The black they were wearing was in mourning over the late king, just like everyone else in the palace that day. But she was sure Maxim didn't have a glimmer of anguish in his heart.

They were walking arm in arm down a long corridor she had never seen before. Following behind many other important looking people, who were probably there to oversee the trial.

Being this close to Maxim made her feel disgusted in herself, and her powerlessness. But she didn't want to upset him now, on the day he was deciding Chilian's fate. It was simply too great of a risk to deny him, even if it killed her inside.

Linari and Sheldy had briefed her on what was about to go down. It wasn't like other trials she had read about before. There was a jury, yes, and a judge. However, it was the judge's call, whether the defendant was guilty or not. The jury would be more like counselors, advising the judge to the best decision. Too bad for them that their judge was King Maxim Istatis II.

They were done for.

When they made it to a giant door probably leading to the courtroom, Maxim took a surprisingly sharp left turn and led her through a door to a room with no windows, and only a few chairs and couches. It was decorated with a chandelier and pieces of expensive art here and there, but nothing else.

Images of previous trials and important events in the court's history hung along the walls. The latest one being King Aldrick sentencing what she believed to be the rebels, all those years ago.

Maxim took a heavy seat in one of the chairs standing up against a wall.

She could feel his predatory gaze follow her as she pretended to study the paintings.

"You haven't spoken a word to me all day, doll. How come?" he asked in a saddened voice. She had no answer she could give him without bad consequences, so she lied, "I'm feeling under the weather, after recent events…" Her voice was weak and believable to make sure she came off as a scared little girl.

"Are you worried for my father's killer?" he asked in an entertained tone.

She thought about it quickly. "From where I stood, it all looked like a freak accident… Wrong place, wrong time. So I don't believe he deserves what becomes of murderers," she explained.

Maxim was quiet for a while as he considered her words. "Is he still like a brother to you, doll?"

The thought made her dizzy, but that was the lie she had bewildered Maxim to keep Chilian as a close attendant, so she had to persevere. "Of course, your Majesty…" she said.

His gaze softened a little as his smile widened. "You are very wise, do you know that? You'll be a wonderful queen."

All air left her lungs as she realized that he had actually meant what he said back in her quarters. Was he going to marry her? Was she going to bear his heirs and live by his side in this place for the rest of her life? Was he just going to make her wear a crown and sit still on a throne like an actual porcelain doll?

"Oh, your Majesty, you can't be serious, can you?" She asked, desperate to find a way to escape that fate, "there are a lot of other, more suitable ladies in this court, who would do a much better job at being queen." she pleaded.

"I know," he said with a laid-back attitude, "but they are all self-obsessed, whores, only in it for the gain. You want nothing to do with me. I find that enticing."

"You're torturing me... That's something completely different..." she mumbled.

A slick laugh was heard from his chair. "You disrespected me, remember? Back at the pond."

"I know, and you punished me! Why keep me like this? I have no value compared to the others." Her tone was becoming dangerous.

"I am the king. A king can have what he wants," he responded plainly. Rage boiled beneath her blood, and she had trouble holding it all back.

"And when you get tired of me? Then what?" she asked.

"I'll keep you here. Locked in your room. Where you can wither like the flower you are."

He was so nonchalant about it. He had no feelings of doubt or regret, or even sympathy. She felt her heart break, piece by piece, as this man turned out to be nothing but an actual monster.

At that moment she wished that flowers could bite.

Suddenly, the door went up again.

Two black figures glided elegantly into the room, completely covered in mournful garments. Sofeel and the now widowed queen Alryn.

Their faces were shadowed by black veils, and their clothes truly made it feel like something bad had happened. For Sofeel to have lost her father on a day of celebration, and for the queen to have watched her beloved husband being cut down in front of her. It must have been maddening, having to publicly appear again already.

And now they had to stand side by side with King Aldrick's real killer, while they were forced to obey his every word.

How could two of the strongest women she knew be broken by the swing of a single sword? Aimee had no answer for it and likely never would have.

"Mother, Sofeel..." Maxim stood up to greet the women, but they both returned the greeting in a deep curtsey instead of the obvious hug Maxim was about to give them. Never had she felt more joy than when she saw Maxim awkwardly acknowledge the fact that his mother down right rejected him. *A small victory*, she thought to herself.

"I didn't think either of you would like to attend an event like this, so soon after his passing," Maxim spun, clearly forcing the sorrow in his voice.

"We came here to ask you for something, your Majesty..." Alryn explained. Aimee could faintly see Sofeel nodding in agreement under her veil. She tried making eye contact, but it was next to impossible.

"What is it?" Maxim asked dryly, like he had been offended and tried to brush it off.

Alryn shook her head. It was like she couldn't find the words, as her lips kept trying to form something of importance. So Sofeel bravely stepped up and took the lead. "We all know what happened was an accident. That Chilian didn't mean to kill Father. And you know it too. Please show him mercy. He doesn't deserve the fate of a killer."

The room was silent.

Maxim had tipped his head down to stare at the ground as he considered her words. As it stretched longer and longer, she could see the fear strike under Sofeel's veil as she had clearly angered him.

Without hesitation or warning, Maxim's hand came flying through the air. A loud slap was heard along with screams from the old queen, as Sofeel was sent crashing to the ground, hitting her head against a chair in the downfall. She landed hard, face down on the floor, where her veil fell off.

"SOFEEL!" Aimee rushed over to see if she was hurt, and she quickly helped the queen turn her over so they could assess the damage made to her friend's face.

"I am the king, and I am in charge!" Maxim yelled at them, from above, "you lowly women have no right to tell me how to treat a murderer, so you'll all be damned if this happens again, you hear me?"

Never before had she heard him shout like that, and it made her bones shake in fear of the man standing above her.

Alryn was crying across from her as she held the semi-conscious Sofeel close in her arms. It had clearly hurt by the look of the red mark left on Sofeel's cheek and the growing blue spot on the place her forehead that had hit the vase on the way down.

"You three are all under my rule, and you are *never* to take that killer's side again, do I make myself clear?" he asked with a voice full of disdain.

Aimee nodded slowly and so did the shaking queen. Maxim's rageful expression faded again to the calm smile he had worn just a moment before. It was interesting how he was able to keep his calm around her but lost his temper completely around his family.

"My doll, leave those two," he said sharply, "they are clearly too distressed to be with us today." He pulled in a little rope that was attached to a bell she hadn't noticed earlier to summon a maid. "Please take these two to their chambers. They are too distraught to take part in court today. Make sure they stay there." he said coldly. The maid nodded and left quickly again. Then a small group of guards entered the room, and escorted the two women out and away. They almost dragged Sofeel. She was left alone on the floor too stunned to do anything but stare at the door they had just left through.

"Doll, come here." she heard Maxim command, this time with annoyance clear in his voice. She tried to pick herself up again, took a deep breath and stood up. Aimee walked over to the monster who had sat back down in his chair. She stood in front of him, and tried to hold back her cries best she could.

He reached out and took a hold of both her good and broken hand. It hurt as he led them to his head and gently buried his face. It stung in the broken hand for a moment, but she didn't say a word.

It was weird holding his head in her hands, and his faint breath felt warm on her skin. "I'm sorry you had to see that, doll…" he whispered into her skin, "I'm just stressed. Being king is very exhausting…" he mumbled.

Aimee looked at him confused. It was rare for him to be so vulnerable in front of her, and she couldn't comprehend how he could go from the monster who hits his sister to a mere man showing human emotions. Her mind was racing a hundred miles an hour, and her heart was going even faster.

A loud bell began ringing throughout the halls outside and a hidden door in the wall flung open. A butler in an unfamiliar uniform informed them of the trial's imminent beginning, and Maxim led out a loud sigh. He stood up without a warning sending her stumbling back and he started walking towards the hidden door.

"All right, let's get this over with," he said as he rather forcefully took a hold of Aimee's arm. She stumbled a little more and stood next to him arm in arm. She realized that to him this was just a bothersome chore that had to be with with. To her, this was life or death.

The butler led them through a narrow hall leading up a flight of stairs and ending in front of a wooden double door. Over the top of the frame, a sentence was carved to remind whoever stepped through the entrance, to make the right decision.

A Just King Will Always Win The Heart Of His People.

It said everything about Maxim as he completely ignored the text and stepped through the door.

Chapter 17

Wait. *What?*

They stepped out onto a big balcony overlooking a grand hall. It looked exactly like the one depicted in the paintings she had studied earlier. Maxim sat down in an old looking chair behind an even older looking desk with neatly organized papers, books, and other utensils. She was instructed to stand right next to him at all times, so that she would always be visible to the people below. And of course be quiet.

She could already feel that the lack of food, the uncomfortable clothes, and her high heels were going to kill her by the end of the day.

Suddenly the bell rang again, and finally the doors closed. They were not to be opened again, till a decision had been made and the final sentence was given.

The large hall was filled with people yelling and screaming at each other, all dressed in black attire for the month-long mourning period King Aldrick's death had brought upon them.

Men and women, crying, discussing, agreeing, and disagreeing over the recent event that shook the calm palace life they all enjoyed to the fullest intent. Aimee hadn't given them a lot of thought as she first arrived at The Withall Keep Palace and had been too removed from the main events to really get a good look at them. But now that she stood above them all, behind Maxim, she realized that they actually were there, and all lived their own lives inside of the giant walls surrounding them. They all had faces and minds, thoughts that she had never considered. They were more than just surnames and titles to study for hours.

And they should all help determine Chilian's fate.

She looked around for familiar faces in the loud crowd. Most of the highly titled nobles like the Archdukes and Duchess', except her father, of course, were assembled at a high table for councilors.

She saw families like the Aestolas, and the Aquils, and she recognized tons of the witnesses that had been present on the night. She didn't remember the names of many of them, as she had a few weeks earlier. The many years of lecturing had all gone to waste as she was too exhausted to connect faces with names. She saw people that had visited their estate in Leirath throughout her life. People she had known but never bothered talking with.

In the crowd she found Sir Colyn and Laurence's comforting faces. They were both looking up at her. They were standing side by side off to the left, Laurence with a stoic smile and Colyn looking confused as to why she was standing by Maxim's side. She managed to send them a reassuring nod, but their expressions didn't change much.

There were a few others, but she couldn't connect their faces to any names.

They were all so loud as they argued about Chilian's innocence. A headache was already forming.

So Maxim did the only sensible thing, of course, which was to draw his sword, and stab directly through the wood of the old desk he was sitting in front of. The old wood crackled under the blades cut, and the sound of it rung throughout the hall. "SILENCE!" he yelled out of nowhere, and with almost no effort silenced all of the racing discussions going around the tables, and grandstands.

Maxim was also silent as he looked out over the room, probably enjoying the complete attention his outburst had given him. He shook his shoulders quickly, pulled his sword from the old wood and began.

"Many of you know me as Crown Prince Maxim Istatis, second of his name, and heir to the throne of Oplia. But now you will know me as King Maxim. A title that has been thrust upon me earlier than any of us had ever expected." He held an artistic pause in his speech to let his words sink in to the people in the gathering. He sounded like a true king. Not posh or happy over the power he had gained, but sincere and strong. Aimee couldn't help but admire his incredible way of acting.

Maxim continued, "Four days ago, at what should have been my father's celebration of his thirteenth year on the throne, he was brutally cut down at the dance. He battled for another hour before he was declared dead by his personal doctor. Many of you saw this act. And many of you did not. But what we all have in common is the loss of a great man. A husband. A Father. A knight. And a king. He was someone to all of us and we are here today to bring some kind of justice to his early death. By punishing the sole person, responsible for the king's end."

Maxim subtly made a hand gesture, signaling one of the guards standing in the middle of the great hall. He quickly ran out to one of the sides and pulled someone out of the shadow of the grandstand. The sound of rattling chains and weak footsteps rung throughout the quiet hall, as he appeared in front of them all.

Aimee couldn't hold back a gasp as Chilian's grimy face became visible through the crowd of people. He was still wearing the exact same clothes as the night of the incident. The long white coat with the golden sleeves and the knee-high boots that had looked so uncomfortable.

He was smeared in dirt and filth, and a big red stain was left on his chest as he had been knocked out and landed in the king's fresh blood. His hair was messy and greasy, and his face looked beaten and tired. He was pale and moved as a rattling skeleton as he walked towards the defendant's booth. But he still tried to stand strong and showcase the little pride he had left.

She felt her heart breaking as she just barely noticed the pearl he had sitting on his neckline, as shiny and clean as the day he was taken away.

Her eyes blurred as she realized how horribly he had been treated and how she had done nothing for him in all of his time in the dungeons.

It took him a second to spot her as he clearly still struggled with the bright light coming in through all of the windows in the back of the hall. But when he finally recognized her, it was like everything paused for him. A brief moment he stopped dead in his tracks, staring up at her as if he had never seen anything like her before. She could've sworn that she saw a faint smile on his lips, before the guard behind him pushed him forward, against the defendant's podium where he was to receive his judgment.

All around them she heard whispering and distasteful words, but she also saw sympathy in many eyes. The hall was clearly divided on their opinion of Chilian. And maybe that was a good thing?

Maxim stood up from his chair again.

"Chilian Malvaria, heir to Stillgate Duchy and now first in line to the throne of Oplia. You are here today under the accusation of murdering the late King Aldrick Istatis. How do you plea?" His voice was loud and powerful, and she got the sense that he had prepared a lot for that delivery.

Chilian looked around for a moment, and again briefly made eye contact with Aimee, before speaking. "I plead innocent!" he responded in a tone that showed off the incredible strength he still held, even after his four-day imprisonment.

Maxim nodded once, and both men sat down on their respective chairs.

"My people! I call upon today's first witness. A girl who stood only a few feet away when it all went down. Lodi Grems' youngest daughter of Marquis Olwin Grems. Please stand and tell us your story," Maxim ordered.

A small girl, no older than fourteen, stood up from one of the grandstands and walked down the stairs to stand in the middle of the hall. Her tanned face was pale and her hair messy. She had clearly been affected by what she had seen that night. *Poor girl*, Aimee thought to herself.

Lodi did a curtsey in front of Maxim and cleared her throat. "I remember that I was standing with my mother, as I heard a loud gasp or a scream maybe. I turned around to see Sir Malvaria and you, your Majesty, arguing over the woman to your side." She did a gesture towards Aimee, and she suddenly felt hundreds of eyes upon her. She had completely forgotten how vital of a point she had been in the entire affair.

She tried not to look bothered by Lodi's words, but it was clear for everyone to see how sick it made her feel.

The girl continued, "Sir Malvaria drew his sword as the scene escalated and I believe the late king had heard it. Because suddenly, he and Queen Alryn stormed over. I think your Majesty was holding the Lady from Sir Malvaria, provoking him enough to try and cut you down. But you stepped aside at the right time, and the slash went to the king's chest. I could be wrong though.

He then collapsed, and all I remember from there on out was pure chaos."

Lodi ended her description of the event, and a whisper started stirring all around them, discussing her statement.

Maxim looked annoyed at the fact that she had called him out specifically but nodded, and she once again curtsied and went back to her seat.

"Thank you Lodi Grems. Next I call upon Cane Wright, Marquis of Ashfield," Maxim said.

At one of the tables on the other side of the hall, an elderly man with dark gray hair, and a long thin beard stood up. He could barely walk, and had to rely on an old walking stick to keep his balance. He looked pathetic as he slowly made his way to the middle of the floor and had to ask for a chair to sit down on, as he was too weak to stand under his statement.

Aimee looked down from the balcony again to see Chilian, not looking at Marquis Wright, but at her. His gaze was soft, and it must have been intentional, because it quickly calmed her. In return she sent back a warm smile, reassuring him that she was on his side in all of this.

Their eye contact was broken however, when Maxim once again spoke. "Marquis Cane Wright. You were with the late king right before the incident. Tell us what happened, exactly."

All mumbling voices died off as the elderly man coughed to clear his throat and began his anecdote. "Me and his late Majesty were chatting about experiences of our younger days. We in particular talked about the days he was newly instated as ruler, like you are now sir," he explained and earned a single nod from Maxim, "well our wives were also chatting, until my dear wife heard the sound of a sword being drawn. She alerted the king immediately, and together he and Queen Alryn rushed over to see what was going on.

Me and my wife were a little farther behind them, as my leg hindered us a fair bit. But we arrived just in time to see your Majesty move aside and the blade being planted in my old friend's flesh. He then fell to the ground, and as sweet Lodi said earlier, everything was chaos from there on out."

The hall again burst out into chatter and discussions, as Cane Wright finished. Maxim quickly thanked him and continued on to the next witness.

The trial continued like that for what felt like an eternity. Getting every single witness's testimony, and every single angle of the story there was.

Some told about how they rushed from the other side of the gathering to get a glimpse of what was happening, others told of the time afterwards and what happened to them when everything had settled down. Some began the story from when they entered the doors of the ballroom and others explained how they had only heard the sounds of the ruckus. All of the stories were almost identical, all painting it as a freak accident, but nobody dared call it Maxim's fault directly.

They all hesitated when it came to how he was the one who had initiated the whole conflict, and how he was the real one to blame in all of this. They were all too afraid of the consequences their words would have if they did, and they were all obviously just trying to save their own skin when talking about him. So that entire part remained completely vague.

Many painted Chilian as the bad guy, but even more painted him as the actual victim of the bad circumstances. By the end of the last statement, Chilian's fate was still rather unclear, and as Aimee had predicted, she felt the extreme fatigue of standing still the entire time, starting to set in.

Sometimes she glanced down at Chilian who looked to be growing more and more concerned each time they made eye contact. She was slowly losing balance as she had stood there for hours without food or water to give her strength. A dizziness had been planted in her head and many faces around her looked concerned and then blurry as she slowly lost grip of reality.

She looked over at Maxim who also stared at her. with a disgusting smile on his face, as if he was enjoying her illness. He wasn't even listening to the statements. They didn't matter to him, because he had already made his decision. She could see it in his cold eyes as he kept staring at her struggling. All of the witnesses were just to make the entire trial seem legit. They were already doomed. It was so obvious.

The last witness finally finished their story and Maxim stood up.

"I have heard all of your stories and all of your views. We will now have a brief recess, so I can compile all of the statements and make the right decision," he said confidentially, "fifteen minutes is all I need, so use this time however you like. But be ready again soon, and remember that the doors will not be opened for anyone." The table of high councilors quietly discussed the short amount of time Maxim had given himself for the final decision, but he simply stood up and walked over to Aimee. Her weak legs made it difficult to stand and she had to support her weight on the stone railing of the balcony. She searched for Chilian one last time before she would be taken away to the monster's lair, but he was already on his way out. He was being escorted to his seat behind one of the grandstands by guard. He just barely managed to look back over his shoulder and they shared one last glimpse of each other, before he was gone. She felt her throat tightening.

"My dear, you look terrible…" Maxim said as he suddenly appeared next to her. He sounded like he was trying to hold back laughter and be sincere.

"I'm sorry…" she managed to say. She crossed her legs to do a curtsey so she could walk away quickly, but the sudden movement was clearly too much for her and she felt her legs stumble and collapse under her.

She fell through the air but didn't hit the floor like she had expected. Instead she felt Maxim's arms around her, keeping her on her feet and supporting her weight. Gasps sounded from beneath them, and guards around them rushed over, but Maxim told them off. Without any effort he scooped her up from the ground and carried her away from the public's view.

It was like his presence completely numbed her. She was too exhausted and frightened to tell him off.

"I guess you're too fragile for my treatment," Maxim whispered into her ear, as he carried her through the door they had entered through. Everything was spinning. Her head was resting on his shoulder, and she could faintly feel his heartbeat through his chest. The fact that he actually had one took her back a little.

They walked down the stairs and ended up in the same room as before. He sat her down in a chair and went over to the small bell and rang it briefly. A maid poked her head through the door to the long hallway. "Lunch please. Just a single plate." he ordered.

Aimee thought she had heard it wrong. Was he ordering food for her? For her to *eat?* Her stomach rumbled at the thought of a royal lunch. He heard it and turned around. "I really hope you aren't finding all of this too bothersome, my dear."

She was too tired to answer him, so he would have to do with a single nod. "You have been very good throughout the entirety of today. There was a bit of a hiccup this morning with my mother and sister, but other than that you have been a good toy," he rambled on, "continue like that and our time together will be very pleasant."

A knock came from the door, and Maxim went over to open it up. A tray with a silver platter was brought into the room and immediately a delicious scent of cooked chicken spread throughout the small room.

Maxim placed the plate on a table in front of her and dismissed the maid that had brought it. He retrieved another chair from a far corner and sat down in front of her. She looked from him to the food, as to have him confirm that it was actually real and not just a beautiful fantasy. He sent her a soft smile, uncanny for his usual behavior, and looked down again. She felt a smile form on her mouth as she inspected the dish further. It looked to be a fried chicken breast with an array of different garnishes like potatoes, celery, carrots, and lots of other things.

But her drooling mouth closed as Maxim's fork pierced through the chicken breast and he started eating it, right in front of her.

The hole inside of her stomach expanded and then crumbled together again in a painfully spiteful feeling. He looked pleased with himself, as her expression said all too well how rageful and desperate she felt in that moment. Her stomach rumbled out of jealousy and the bitterness of his smug smile while he was enjoying the delicious meal, was enough to drive her insane. For a while she just stared shocked at the fork moving from the meat to his mouth and back again.

To think that she actually thought he would do something so nice for her was laughable. *How could she have been so naive?*

After a while all there was left was a bit of the garnish, and maybe one fourth of the chicken.

He placed down the fork and knife and looked her in the eyes. She felt like if she tried hard enough she could make him burn through her mere glare, but nothing happened to his annoying smile.

"Doll, I noticed that you were looking a bit hungry earlier," he finally said after minutes of silence. "This is a big trial for both of us, so you should have all the strength you require. Please." He gestured towards the already eaten meal. "Take all you want. We'll be continuing in four minutes time."

Her jaw dropped as she realized that he was making her eat his leftovers. He stood up. "Better hurry, doll." He left out of the hidden door in the wall and a guard replaced him, ready to escort her back out to the balcony.

She looked down at the remaining food and damned herself internally. Then she picked up the used fork, dried it off in a tissue she had in her pocket, and started eating the sad leftovers. She hated to admit how heavenly it tasted, after all those weeks with nothing but fruit and bread. The seasoning was perfect, and the moist texture made it feel like the meat was melting on her tongue. Oh how she had missed a hot meal. The garnish had been fried in some kind of delicious sauce in it all mixed together to the best meal she had had maybe all of her life.

The guard from the corner cleared his throat. "My Lady, it is time to return…"

She stopped midway through a bite. She wasn't done eating yet. Would she just have to leave the rest, and survive on those few bites she had managed to come by?

"Just one minute…?" she asked, but the guard shook his head, and stood, ready to guide her through the small hallway.

She felt the tears pressing, but this wasn't the time. To believe she wished to eat more, than to be by Chilian's side was absurd. She shook her head, disgusted by herself.

So she put down the fork and knife. Dried off her mouth and walked over to the guard. She would stand tall in there. Ready for whatever the outcome would be. If Chilian was deemed to be killed, she would stand by his side. She would cast herself on the chopping board too if necessary.

She didn't want to be the reason for his death without sacrificing something too.

She would die by his side if necessary.

*

The guard that was with him was one of the older guys he had worked with. They had talked and trained together, and he was a pretty nice guy. They had had great conversations before the mess he was in, and now he was just happy that a familiar face was responsible for him.

In fact he was a friend to most of the guards around the castle and he understood that most of them were on his side. They had never liked Maxim, and all knew him as a liar and a spoiled brat. Chilian was glad to have the greatest force in the palace behind him in this.

Finally the bell rung again, signaling the end of the short recess. Everyone had already taken their seats and now it was Chilian's turn to make his grand entrance, once again.

Or as grand as it could be while he smelled like a dirty stable.

His clothes were so disgusting and his brown hair was greasier than after most of his training sessions with Laurence or Colyn.

It was a little embarrassing to be showcased in such a state, but it also revealed the terrible conditions the Keepers held the captives in. So maybe it would set more focus on prisoner's wellbeing? No, probably not. None of these people cared for lowly nothings like those in the dungeons. He had been exactly like them a few days ago, so who was he to talk?

However, one he knew would care was Aimee, who stood steady and strong on the balcony as he turned the corner. Just a few moments earlier she had been on the brink of fainting, extremely pale, sick-looking and just seemed like someone who shouldn't have been outside a meter radius of a bed. But something had changed. She looked down at him with calm and comforting eyes. Her flaming hair glittering in the sunlight coming in through the giant windows and a sturdy posture. She was no longer as pale, and she looked determined. She looked beautiful.

He wondered what would have made such a significant change over the course of fifteen short minutes. What had she witnessed behind those doors, and what had Maxim said to her, to make her so steadfast?

He felt the small pearl burn against his chest, calling her to him, and he longed to see those brave eyes up front. Touch her soft cheek and do whatever comes next *together*. Not separated by the stone railing and the five-meter drop between them.

His eyes turned away from her and searched out into the crowd for his parents. His mother was sitting on one of the grandstands looking as distraught as ever. She had always been loving towards him and he couldn't imagine the pain she felt seeing her one and only son on trial for the murder of her brother. Was she disappointed? Was that what she was feeling?

He couldn't bear looking at her, as he already knew the

answer, so he turned his attention to the high council. He had been up there lots of times with his father, to practice the work of a counselor. He had assisted both him and King Aldrick in many decisions over the years, and now that he was the one on trial he knew exactly how little impact their advice would have on today's outcome.

His father was looking at him. Those green eyes. He had been a strict Father, yes, but also just. Had Chilian worked a good days' worth, he was rewarded greatly. If he had achieved any new rank or skill he was praised, and over all they had a good relationship. He wondered if that would continue after all of this was over.

He couldn't determine his look. He never could. Was he angry or disappointed? Sad or worried? There really was no telling.

Once again he decided to turn away, ashamed of what he had brought down upon his family's name.

Finally there was Maxim. The snake. The monster and now the king. His prosecutor and his judge. The mere boy that was to rule the kingdom and decide his fate.

He was smiling as always, with his hair slicked back and the black suit showcasing his supposed mourning. If he had just been a little quicker that day, maybe they would have been at Maxim's funeral right now.

Chilian finally walked up to the defendant's podium and sat down like the rest of the nobles.

Maxim stood up.

He was nothing but a child with too much power.

"My people. I have reached a conclusion on Sir Chilian Malvaria's sentence," he paused. "But before announcing it I would like to call upon one last witness." A mumbling discussion broke out immediately as this unexpected delay of Chilian's death sentence was a shock to all.

He made eye contact with his cousin. Two pairs of Istatis cyes, burning equally murderous. Chilian felt his hands tightening into fists in his shackles.

Maxim turned to look out over the nobles again. "Beware that I already have made my decision. Nothing will impact it, from here on out. So whatever our witness decides to say is completely irrelevant to the final sentence." The mumbling quieted down and the silence was almost unbearable. "I call Aimee Achillea."

An audible gasp sounded throughout the hall and all eyes flew towards his Blossom, who looked just as confused and taken aback as the rest of the people there. "Aimee Achillea, second daughter of Archduke Erlan Achillea. You were a vital part of this entire incident, so it would only be fair to hear your version of the story as well. So please. What happened on the night of my father's death?" Maxim's eyes were piercing through her.

Chilian knew what he was doing. It was a trap for her. If she didn't call him out for starting the entire ruckus it would be a bigger reason to put the blame on Chilian. If she did call him out, Maxim was sure to make her life a living hell, when Chilian was gone. It was a double-edged sword. He felt his fists clench even further. She shouldn't have to be put on a pedestal like that, exposed to everyone there.

Her eyes found him in the chaos. They were filled with confusion and fear. What he wouldn't do to jump up there and kidnap her. Right then and there, out of the window next to her, down the stone wall and flea to the small mansion in Chission. *Maybe he would take out Maxim on the way?*

But none of that was a good or even possible feat so all he

could do now was nod at her, giving Aimee all the courage he could from down there. He just had to hope she would say the right thing to save her own skin.

*

His comforting eyes were all she needed at that moment. Probably all she ever would need. She nodded back to him and turned her head to face Maxim. He was waiting patiently like everyone else in the hall.

She took a deep breath.

"On the night of the king's death, I was with Sir Malvaria the entire evening. Many of you probably recall us dancing with all of the other royals." A conjoined nodding spread throughout the room as they all remembered the magical moment her and Chilian shared.

"Afterwards we were having a drink together when I felt a pull of my hair. His Majesty was holding me at knifepoint and Sir Chilian was calmly trying to talk him from doing anything reckless."

She could see Maxim's smile turn more and more spiteful as she exposed him to the rest of the gathering. It felt good. He had expected her to be frightful and timid, given the sudden chance to talk freely. But his taunting of her hunger earlier was gonna cost him. She looked down at Chilian who was staring at her in disbelief. "As the situation escalated and my life was increasingly put into danger, Sir Malvariadrew his sword, simply wanting to protect me. As you can see here," Aimee pointed to the cut on her cheek. "His Majesty's knife did in fact cut through my skin, giving Sir Malvariathe signal that he had to strike before I was hurt further. It just so happened, that the late king had heard the ruckus and rushed over to stop anyone from getting killed. Sir Malvaria struck out after King Maxim, but he dodged it. I didn't see what happened specifically, but I remember the late king falling to the floor and Sir Malvaira getting knocked out."

She bowed to Maxim and stepped back on the balcony, but the crowd didn't break out into any kind of mumbling or discussion. She had said what everyone else was too afraid to acknowledge. She was definitely going to pay for it later, but at least now, she had one up on the king of Oplia.

It felt good.

She looked over at him.

His eyes were staring at her with a murderous look.

He finally turned back to the rest of the assembly.

The silence was broken by him clearing his throat and standing up. "Thank you, my Dear. It was a testimony much different than most others but as I promised, none of your words will have an impact on what will happen to Sir Chilian Malvaria. And now if you would let me, I will give my cousin the sentence he deserves."

She looked down at Chilian. He was staring nervously at Maxim. His glance briefly flew over her eyes and then back again. She felt her stomach tossing and turning, and she was sure the small bites she had taken earlier were on their way up again.

Maxim looked down on his cousin.

"Chilian Malvaria, heir to Stillgate and first in line to the throne—" he held a pause for dramatic effect and the silence was almost as loud as someone screaming in her ear.

"I deem you n*ot* guilty."

All air left her lungs.

Wait. *What?*